"Do you want me to go?"

Nick was so still Kika thought she'd done something wrong. He opened his eyes and what Kika saw made her tremble.

"No, I don't want you to go," he said, his breath hot against her face. "I want you to stay so that I can show you that I know how to have fun."

"And how do you plan to do that?" she asked with a provocative push of her hips against his.

His answer made her forget all the reasons she wasn't supposed to get involved with him. Made her forget he wasn't the man she should have wanted. But he was the man she wanted to feel inside her. The man she needed to feel inside her. She savored every moment of the ecstasy, wishing it would never end.

But it did, and later, as he lay propped on one elbow, he said, "That wasn't fun, Kika." She would have turned away from him, but he placed a hand along her jaw and added, "That was uncontrollable desire." He placed kisses on her forehead, her nose, her mouth, and then with slow deliberation caressed her swollen breasts. "Fun is what comes next."

Pamela Muelhbauer is acknowledged as the author of this work.

ISBN 0-373-82556-0

FANCY'S BABY

PAMELA BAUER

Fancy's Baby

She came to Tyler looking
for a baby.
And she found a man.

Harlequin Books

TORONTO • NEW YORK • LONDON
AMSTERDAM • PARIS • SYDNEY • HAMBURG
STOCKHOLM • ATHENS • TOKYO • MILAN
MADRID • WARSAW • BUDAPEST • AUCKLAND

WELCOME TO A
HOMETOWN REUNION

Twelve books set in Tyler.
Twelve unique stories. Together they form a
colorful patchwork of triumphs and trials—
the fabric of America's favorite hometown.

Unexpected Son **Marisa Carroll**
September '96

The Reluctant Daddy **Helen Conrad**
October '96

Love and War **Peg Sutherland**
November '96

Hero in Disguise **Vicki Lewis Thompson**
December '96

Those Baby Blues **Helen Conrad**
January '97

Daddy Next Door **Ginger Chambers**
February '97

A Touch of Texas **Kristine Rolofson**
March '97

Fancy's Baby **Pamela Bauer**
April '97

Undercover Mom **Muriel Jensen**
May '97

Puppy Love **Ginger Chambers**
June '97

Hot Pursuit **Muriel Jensen**
July '97

Mission: Children **Marisa Carroll**
August '97

Around the quilting circle...

"I do love this pattern," Tessie Finklebaum declared, looking down at the stars and stripes of the quilt stetched out before her in its walnut frame.

"Liza thinks we ought to call it Independence. She says it reminds her of the Fourth of July," said Martha Bauer as she worked her needle through the fabric.

"And she's right," Annabelle Scanlon stated authoritatively. "I think we ought to raffle it off at the picnic." Much of the quilting circle's work was either donated to charity or raffled off for a worthy cause.

"I hear they're bringing in a carnival this year," Bea Ferguson remarked.

Annabelle sighed. "Don't I know it. My two grandsons have talked about nothing else."

"And Melody?" Tessie asked gently.

Annabelle shot her a warning look. "Melody hasn't said anything."

Her statement was greeted with a chorus of sympathetic "oh's." Everyone in Tyler knew how concerned Annabelle was that her granddaughter was nearly two years old and had yet to utter a single word. They'd all hoped that when Annabelle enrolled her in TylerTots, the little girl would overcome her shyness—if shyness was what kept Melody from speaking....

CHAPTER ONE

"OH, GOOD. She comes bearing gifts." Propping her two-year-old son on her hip, Frannie Mancini held the screen door open for her sister-in-law.

With a box of chocolates in one hand and a bottle of white zinfandel in the other, Kika Mancini stepped inside the house.

"What are we celebrating?" Frannie asked.

"The fact that I made it out of the studio with my sanity," Kika answered, giving her nephew, T.J., an affectionate tap on the nose.

"Lucky me. Your bad days mean I get wine and chocolate. Today must have been pretty bad," Frannie concluded, eyeing the size of the box.

T.J., recognizing the candy in his aunt's hands, squealed in delight. His tiny fists opened and closed in anticipation of what was inside the cellophane-wrapped package.

Wearing a bib-front denim jumper, with her blond hair pulled back in a ponytail, Kika looked much younger than her twenty-eight years as she ripped open the box of chocolates.

"It's a good thing I left when I did," she said tiredly. "I don't know what would have happened if I had to listen to one more pushy mother try to convince me her child will do whatever is necessary to be a star."

"You're not still looking for the hot dog kids, are you?" Frannie asked, trying to distract T.J. with a soda cracker.

Kika sighed. "I haven't found a single one who can sing that hokey hot dog jingle to Mr. Gunther's satisfaction." She studied the assortment of chocolates, then plucked a square piece from the box. Before popping it into her mouth, she added, "Every time I work with kids I have trouble. It's a good thing I'm not a mom."

"It's different when they're your own," Frannie assured her. "Someday you'll see."

Kika knew she should contradict her sister-in-law, but she was in no mood to discuss the subject of motherhood, especially not with anyone connected to her family. None of the Mancinis knew the reason why she was never going to be a mother. And they never would.

"Well, someday isn't here, and in the meantime I have to not only find the hot dog kid, but the Fancy baby, too."

"You're talking about a toddler for the baby-furniture ad?"

Kika nodded. "Horace Fancy wants me to find the perfect baby, which we both know is impossible."

"Yeah, there's only one perfect child in this world and unfortunately, he's not a girl." Frannie made little sucking sounds up and down T.J.'s arm that caused him to giggle.

The display of affection brought a lump to Kika's throat. A familiar cold sensation squeezed her heart. It lasted only a few moments, then disappeared. Nonetheless, it was there, just as it always was whenever she saw a mother hugging her baby. It wasn't envy so much as a sickening sense of loss, a reminder of precious moments she had never had with a daughter she had never known.

With practiced discipline, Kika pushed aside the haunting memory and said, "Tell me what I can do to help with dinner."

"Why don't you take T.J. into the family room so he can watch his new video?" Frannie suggested. "I'll work the kitchen."

Kika grimaced. "Not the singing elephant again."

"No, and you won't need to do any counting or reciting of the alphabet, either. I promise. This video is rather unique."

Kika cast a dubious glance in her sister-in-law's direction.

"Really. It will make you smile."

"So will this." Kika reached for a chocolate cream and eyed it appreciatively before taking a bite.

"That's fattening. The video isn't."

"Wouldn't T.J. rather listen to some music? I've got a new blues CD."

Frannie thrust a hand to her hip. "Uh-oh. That must mean you broke up with Frankie. What happened?"

"He wanted to get married."

"And what's wrong with marriage?"

Kika could see every dark hair on her sister-in-law's head rise defensively. "Nothing. Frankie's what's wrong."

Frannie laughed. "Come. Follow me. I want to show you something." She led Kika to the family room and gestured for her to take a seat on the striped sofa while she turned on the television.

"I'm really not in the mood to watch videos," Kika pleaded.

"This one's different." Frannie's slightly over-weight figure bent to slide the videocassette into the VCR. Within seconds the blank screen was filled with children T.J.'s age.

"What is this?" Kika asked, as two little boys built a tower of blocks.

"It's the latest in baby-sitting tools. It's called Video Playmates," Frannie announced grandly. "When I slip this tape in, T.J. thinks he's at a day-care center playing with other kids. Isn't it neat?"

Kika stared at the TV screen, watching two children roll a big red ball back and forth. "You mean someone actually makes videos of kids playing?"

"Umm-hmm. T.J. loves it. It's like having friends over to play, yet I don't have the hassle of watching someone else's kids. And you should hear the funny things these kids say."

Moments later a little boy in the video tugged on the crotch of his jeans, saying, "Something itches."

Frannie hooted, while Kika simply lifted her eyebrows. "Quite a creative scriptwriter," she said dryly.

"Oh, it's not scripted. That's what makes it all so funny. Everything is natural. Clever, huh?"

Kika didn't want to tell her sister-in-law that to someone who had spent the day interviewing six- and seven-year-olds, watching an unrehearsed video of children at play was not entertainment. It was punishment. She leaned her head back, her eyes drifting shut.

Frannie noticed. "You think it's boring."

Kika tried to look alert. "No, it's a great idea for T.J. It's obvious he likes it," she observed, as her nephew stood transfixed in front of the TV.

"Here. Let me fast-forward it. There's a playmate for moms, too." Frannie pressed a button on the VCR, and tiny bodies moved in frenetic motion. When the tape finally resumed normal speed, she said, "Check this out."

This section of the video didn't look to be much different than the rest, but Kika didn't comment on the fact. Frannie appeared to be just as engrossed with the video as T.J.

"Look at the guy who just walked in the door. Talk about hunk power," Frannie enthused, as a dark-haired man wearing a white shirt and a navy-blue tie looked directly into the camera.

"He's not bad," Kika answered nonchalantly, not wanting to admit that there was something about the man's strong features that caused her muscles to tense in a purely sensual way.

"Not bad? He's great! Too bad Fancy's not looking for a father model. I bet this guy could sell a lot of baby furniture. After all, it's mothers who do the buying."

"Maybe. Who do you suppose he is?" Kika asked, intrigued by the man, whose cheeks dimpled when he smiled.

"I don't think he'd be wearing a suit if he were one of the day-care workers, and he's only in this part of the video."

"He looks like he should be flying a plane or climbing a mountain."

"He is one tall, dark and handsome dude," Frannie said dreamily.

"He's good-looking, but he could be really short. After all, he's in the land of three-foot-tall people," Kika reminded her.

"Maybe he's one of the kids' father."

"More likely a plant to get women to buy the tape," Kika said cynically. "Sex sells everything—even kids' videos."

Frannie clicked her tongue. "You've been in the business too long. You can't even appreciate a good-looking guy anymore."

"Because I've discovered that most good-looking men have no personality." In her work as a casting director, Kika came into contact with gorgeous men on a regular basis. She had learned, however, that the contents weren't necessarily as attractive as the fancy packaging. She knew better than to expect the inner man would be as wonderful as the outer.

"Kuck!" T.J. roared, as one little boy pushed a big red fire engine across the floor, blubbering motorlike sounds.

"Yes, darling, I see the truck," Frannie said to him, then looked back at Kika and added, "See? It's perfect for T.J." Once again she gave her attention to her son and said in a sugary voice, "All the little kids are having fun at play."

"Not all of them," Kika noted. "There's one little girl pouting in the corner."

"You're right. I hadn't noticed her before. Maybe she's camera shy."

"She doesn't look frightened to me. She looks mad." Kika stared at the tiny red-haired girl who stood with lower lip extended, forehead wrinkled.

"Even pouting she's adorable, Look how tiny she is compared to the other children," Frannie commented. "You don't suppose the good-looking guy's her father, do you? She keeps gazing in his direction."

"If he is, he's not acting like it, although he does seem to be tossing furtive glances her way, doesn't he?" Kika leaned forward, her eyes narrowing. "Where's your remote control?"

"It's right next to you on the end table," Frannie answered. "Why?"

Kika picked up the remote and punched several buttons.

"What are you doing?" Frannie shrieked in alarm.

"I'm adjusting the color. I want to see if her hair is really that glorious shade of red or if the color on your set needs to be fine-tuned."

Frannie grabbed the device from Kika's fingers. "You can't do that. Tony has a fit if anyone messes with those function buttons."

Kika snatched it right back and said, "I'll reset it the way it was. My brother won't even know I messed with it."

She adjusted the contrast, color and tint, then said with a satisfied sigh, "That little girl has the most wonderfully expressive face. Where's the video package?"

"I'll get it for you." Frannie retrieved the case from the oak cabinet and handed it to Kika, who quickly scanned the small print on the back. "What are you looking for?"

"The producer's name. It says here this was filmed in Tyler, Wisconsin. Where's that?"

Frannie shrugged. "I never heard of it. I ordered the tape from a catalog."

"Thank goodness you did."

"Are you thinking that little redhead could be Fancy's Baby?" Frannie asked as Kika replayed the portion of the video where the child appeared.

"She's cute and Mr. Fancy's partial to redheads. And there's something about her that makes you want to watch her whether she's pouting or not."

"But she doesn't look like she'd be easy to work with. She won't even play with the other kids in the video," Frannie noted.

"That doesn't mean she wouldn't be a good model. The only way to find out is to test her. I have an idea." Kika pulled a cellular phone from her purse and punched in seven numbers. "Wendy, it's me. Locate Tyler, Wisconsin, for me, will you? And see if you can find out the best way to get there."

"You're going to go to Wisconsin?" Frannie asked as soon as Kika had hung up the phone.

"I might be." She stared pensively at the video package.

"But there are nearly three million people right here in the Minneapolis–St. Paul area. You don't need to go to a small town to find a talent."

Kika didn't comment, but sat tapping her pen against the video package.

"You're serious about this, aren't you?" Frannie stared at her sister-in-law in amazement.

"Horace Fancy has been harping at me to find a model who looks like she's the baby next door. What better place to look for that innocence than in a small town?"

"So you're going to go to Tyler, Wisconsin, and see how many of these babies you can convince to come to Minnesota for an audition?"

Kika nodded. "If these videos are produced on a regular basis, there could be other babies for me to audition as well."

"When will you go?"

"As soon as possible. Horace Fancy wants to launch a huge advertising campaign this fall. If I don't find the right baby, he'll go somewhere else."

Kika's cellular phone rang. Grabbing it up, she quickly pulled a notepad from her purse and began scribbling. As soon as the conversation ended, she said to Frannie, "Sorry, but I can't stay for dinner. I have to go home and pack. I'm leaving tonight."

"You have to be kidding! This commercial can't be that important."

Kika stuffed her notepad back in her purse. "I don't want to lose out on this one. Besides, I've learned in this business that she who hesitates is lost."

"What if that little redhead's mother doesn't want her to be a model?"

"With the kind of incentive Mr. Fancy's offering, she will," Kika answered confidently. "I'll explain that the money she'll earn will make a nice college fund. No mother in her right mind would turn down a chance for her kid to make big bucks in such a short time."

Frannie didn't look convinced. "I'm not so sure about that."

"Well, then it'll be my job to persuade her," Kika stated positively. She bent down to give her nephew a kiss. "Bye, T.J. Have fun."

Frannie followed her to the door. "Maybe you'll meet that hunk in the suit."

Kika could see that her sister-in-law's imagination was running wild. "And if I do, what should I tell him? That there's a married woman back here in Minnesota lusting after his body?''

Frannie clicked her tongue. ''Kika, you're hopeless.''

''I have a job to do.''

''And if you don't find Fancy's Baby? What then?''

''At least I'll know where Tyler, Wisconsin is if the question ever comes up in Trivial Pursuit,'' Kika called over her shoulder as she hurried to her car.

''MELODY THREW her carrots on the floor,'' six-year-old Patrick Miller announced calmly.

''I knew she wouldn't eat them. She hates 'em,'' nine-year-old Zachary said in an I-told-you-so voice.

''Her eyes are gonna go bad.''

''I think she's going to get rickets.''

''What are rickets?''

''You wouldn't understand. You're only six.''

''She's not going to get rickets.'' Annabelle Scanlon's booming voice silenced the boys' chatter. ''Nor will she have bad eyesight because she doesn't eat her carrots.''

The two brothers exchanged dubious glances.

''What's that?'' Zachary asked as his grandmother scooped a serving of her prizewinning tuna hot dish onto his plate.

''It's tuna casserole.''

Zachary eyed it suspiciously. ''Melody's not going to like it.''

''Don't you worry about your sister,'' Annabelle advised, spooning a smaller portion into a bowl decorated with purple dinosaurs. As soon as she set down the dish, Melody shoved it to the edge of the high-chair tray.

"Maybe you should make her a peanut butter samwich," Patrick suggested.

"We all eat the same dinner in this house," Annabelle stated in no uncertain terms. To Melody she said, "Grandma made this hot dish especially for you. Won't you try it?"

There was no response from her granddaughter.

Zach's fork poked at a piece of macaroni on his plate. "Does this have mushrooms in it?"

"What's wrong with mushrooms?" Annabelle demanded.

"I don't like them."

"They're good for you. They're brain food," Annabelle told him, moving to the refrigerator to get a carton of milk.

Zachary wrinkled his nose and Patrick rolled his eyes. Melody took one more look at the noodle concoction before her and with a quick swipe sent it flying.

"Melody threw her food on the floor!" Patrick exclaimed.

Annabelle slammed the refrigerator door with a bang and gave her granddaughter a look that had the power to make even the crankiest of postal patrons cower. Twenty-two-month-old Melody didn't so much as move a muscle. She sat in her high chair with her eyebrows knit, her lower lip pushed out in a pout.

"I knew she wouldn't like it," Zachary stated matter-of-factly. "Dad makes her French toast when she doesn't like what we're having."

"She needs more in her diet than French toast and peanut butter sandwiches," Annabelle declared as the boys exchanged guarded glances. "Your father has spoiled her."

"Dad says she'll develop a taste for other foods as she gets bigger," Zachary said in a tone that reminded Annabelle of her son-in-law.

"Not if your father doesn't start providing you kids with a balanced diet," she warned. Nutrition was one of the many subjects about which she and her son-in-law had a difference of opinion.

Annabelle was well aware of the mistakes Nick Miller had made in raising her grandchildren. In the short time they had been in her care, she had seen more than enough to convince her that as loving and attentive as Nick was, he needed someone to give him a few pointers on parenthood. Annabelle figured she was just the one to take on the task.

It wasn't going to be easy. Having her grandchildren come stay with her until their father completed moving arrangements had already proved to be a mixed blessing. She loved having them under her roof, yet at that same time it pained her to see them in such of state of need.

For they were needy. It was as plain as the nose on her face. What Melody, Zachary and Patrick needed was a mother. Since her son-in-law was in no hurry to do anything about providing one, they would get the next best thing—a grandmother's influence. It was a job Annabelle did not take lightly. She only wished that she had followed her instincts and demanded that Nick bring the children home when Beth had died, nearly two years ago.

Annabelle looked at the three redheads gathered around the kitchen table and felt a rush of sympathy. Their loss had been just as great as hers. At the time of her daughter's death Annabelle had been so consumed by her own grief she hadn't protested Nick's decision to remain in California. But that was over. No longer was she going to be a long-distance grandma.

She poured each of her grandsons a glass of milk, then grabbed several quilted paper towels and attacked the mess on the floor. Next she spooned a small amount of the tuna dish—a casserole she had made from scratch and baked in the oven in spite of the ninety-degree heat—into a clean bowl.

"Melody, Grandma wants you to eat a little of this. It's good for you." Annabelle set the bowl on the high-chair tray beside a double-handled cup.

A chubby little hand pushed the bowl to the edge of the tray.

There was a battle of wills as wide green eyes met narrowed blue ones. Annabelle could feel the green ones winning and consequently said, "Don't throw it on the floor or Grandma will have to send you to bed without any ice cream."

A threat. Annabelle wasn't proud of the tactic, but it had worked when Melody's mother had sat in that very same high chair.

But one thing Annabelle had discovered was that Melody's similarity to her mother ended with the red locks and green eyes. In temperament she was nothing like Beth.

When Melody heard she wasn't going to get any ice cream, her lower lip began to quiver. Before Annabelle could sit down to the dinner table, the tuna was on the floor again and the pout had become a howl.

"That's it, Melody. No ice cream for you." Annabelle wagged a finger at the screaming toddler. Her dictum only caused the howling to escalate.

Zachary spoke up in his sister's defense. "Dad says food shouldn't be a reward or a punishment."

His comment produced a look from Annabelle that had him sinking lower in his chair and eyeing the tuna on his own plate as if it were a life preserver. Melody continued to wail and once again cleared her tray with a swipe of her chubby little arm. Milk and several green grapes joined the food on the floor.

Annabelle decided it was time to change tactics. She would ignore her granddaughter's temper tantrum, for that was what it had become. She sat down and asked Zachary to pass her the butter. He complied.

The howling grew louder, but Annabelle refused to look in Melody's direction. In the short time she had been in Tyler, Melody hadn't uttered one single word. Annabelle knew from experience that the average two-year-old's vocabulary was limited, but Melody had none. Several of Annabelle's friends had commented on her lack of speech. Even the staff at TylerTots had said she was exceptionally quiet for her age. The only one who didn't seem to be concerned was her own father.

But then Nick Miller wasn't overly concerned about any of his children. It was another of those parental points Annabelle intended to share with her son-in-law. He needed a more hands-on approach when it came to Melody. Nick's philosophy in raising children was not to have a plan, to just do whatever needed to be done and expect that things would work out for the best.

Annabelle knew that when it came to Melody, a plan was needed. That was why when Patrick said, "Grandma, I think she's turning purple," she switched to plan C.

This was a battle Annabelle did not want to lose, yet the tiny little veins in Melody's head did look as though they might burst. No longer did the tears sound like those of a strong-willed child approaching the terrible twos, but rather the painful plea of a motherless little girl who needed love more than she needed discipline. She had slipped down in the high chair so that her splotchy red face was all that was visible.

Annabelle quickly extracted Melody from the chair and cradled her in her arms, murmuring words of comfort. "There, there now, Melody. Grandma doesn't care if you don't eat the tuna. Just quit crying so you don't make yourself sick." Zachary and Patrick exchanged knowing glances.

"One of you boys get me the peanut butter from the cupboard," she instructed, reaching for a slice of white bread from the plate in the center of the table.

Patrick dutifully got up, which suited Zachary just fine. With his grandmother preoccupied with Melody and Patrick away from the table, he was able to slip his mushrooms into his napkin. It was a feat he accomplished with the ease of a magician performing a sleight-of-hand trick.

Annabelle, Zachary and Patrick ate the tuna casserole. Melody ate her peanut-butter sandwich. All four of them had chocolate chip ice cream for dessert.

By the time her grandchildren were tucked in bed, Annabelle was exhausted. Only one thought saved her from slinking into a blue funk: tomorrow their father would be here.

NICK MILLER ZIPPED the last suitcase shut, then looked around the empty room. Everything was gone—the four-poster bed he and Beth had slept in for thirteen years, the chest of drawers that had held her clothes, the oak shelves that had been filled with figurines she had painted in her weekly ceramics classes.

All the familiar rooms where he and Beth had laughed together, slept together and even wept together were now empty—just like him. In the first few months after her death he had tried to keep everything just as she had left it, but that had been impossible. Her house plants had turned brown, the highly polished floors had become scuffed and the brightly colored linens had faded. Instead of finding comfort in the knowledge that she had loved fixing up the three-bedroom rambler, he could only feel pain that she was no longer there.

That was why, when his mother-in-law had pleaded with him to move the children closer to her, he had finally agreed it was time he left the house in Sherman Oaks, California and all of its memories. The one-day-at-a-time approach hadn't worked. He needed a fresh start.

The problem was he wasn't sure that settling in the town where Beth had been born and raised was going to help him move forward with his life. It would, however, give his children a chance to get to know their grandmother and the rest of the Scanlon family, who lived in the small Midwestern town of Tyler, Wisconsin.

For someone who had spent all his life on the West Coast, living in the middle of America would be quite a change. The first time Nick visited Tyler he had been charmed by the nineteenth-century flavor of its architecture. There was something about the white-framed Victorian homes with their large porches and velvet-green lawns that was refreshingly peaceful compared to the concrete congestion of L.A.

Of course, whenever he had visited Tyler Beth had been with him. Now he was going back alone, and he wasn't sure it would hold the same appeal. For that reason, instead of buying a house, he had rented a smaller version of the grand Victorian homes on Elm Street. It was a two-story with a porch, and a white picket fence that meant Melody could play outside and he wouldn't have to worry about her wandering away.

At the thought of his daughter, his breath caught in his throat. He closed his eyes and fought back a familiar wave of guilt. Melody was the daughter he had always wanted, the third child he had insisted they have and the true reason he was moving to Tyler.

Something was badly broken in his relationship with Melody, something that needed to be put right. Professionals had assured him that in time he would bond with the little girl, whose life had begun when his wife's had ended. So far that hadn't happened. In less than six weeks she would be two years old, yet he still felt like a new father with her.

Annabelle insisted that what all his children needed at this point in time was a woman's touch. Nick wouldn't argue that Melody needed a mother, only he wasn't quite sure how he could make that happen.

The thought of dating held no interest for him. No woman could replace Beth. There was no point in looking for love.

There was only one thing to do. He would go to Tyler, give the kids the chance to get to know their grandmother. She was the next best thing to having a mother, even if she did sound a bit like a female General Patton at times. Beneath the tough exterior there had to be a gentle woman. After all, Annabelle had raised Beth and Cece, women Nick admired for their gentleness.

Actually, he looked forward to raising his children in a town that wasn't populated with surgically assisted bodies. When he'd been younger it hadn't bothered him that people in Tinseltown reshaped their body parts as often as they redecorated their houses. Lately, however, he had grown tired of living in the shadow of the glittery entertainment industry.

It was time to leave. He lifted his suitcases and looked one last time at the empty room. As he left the sprawling rambler he didn't look back. The time had come to move forward and hope that he would find peace of mind in a town called Tyler.

CHAPTER TWO

"PAPA! WHAT ARE YOU doing here?" Kika's mouth dropped open at the sight of her father standing outside her apartment door.

"I stopped by to see how you are." He glanced over her shoulder and saw the suitcase standing in the hallway. "You're not flying off to L.A. again, are you?"

"No."

"Good." He grunted as he walked past her. "Your mother will be happy to hear that. When you're in California you seem to forget you have a family in Minnesota."

"I could never forget you and Mama," Kika assured him. "This is a business trip, Papa." She tossed several legal-size pads into her briefcase and snapped it shut. "I need to hurry."

"You're always in a hurry, Kika." He sighed and shoved his hands into his pockets. "A woman shouldn't travel alone. Where's Frankie, anyway?"

Frankie Donato was one of her father's employees, a hardworking, first-generation Italian like her father, with very definite ideas about what women should and shouldn't do. Kika knew that despite her parents' matchmaking attempts, Frankie would never be a member of the family. He wanted a wife who would stay at home and have babies. That wasn't in Kika's future.

"I can't ask Frankie to come with me."

"Why not? Just because you turned down his marriage proposal doesn't mean he's stopped caring about you."

She knew that what her father said was true. Frankie had made it perfectly clear that he would wait for her to get what he called her "independent streak" out of her system. The problem was she didn't want him waiting.

"Frankie has a job," she reminded him.

"I'm the boss. I'll give him tomorrow off." He reached for the phone, but Kika stopped him.

"It's not a good idea. This is business."

He raked a hand through dark hair peppered with gray. "That's what bothers me—this business you're in. Here you are, flying off to who-knows-where in the middle of the night. You're starting to act just like Lucia. No wonder your mother's worried about you."

Lucia—or Lucy, as Kika called her—was her mother's sister. The head of a modeling agency, she had never married or had children, much to the rest of the family's disapproval. To Kika, she was a mentor, a woman to be admired for surviving in an industry that often chewed women up and spat them out again. To Kika's parents, she was a woman to be pitied.

"Aunt Lucy's a successful woman," Kika stated firmly in the woman's defense.

"And a lonely one. Which is what you're going to be if you're not careful." He wagged a finger at her.

"I'm not lonely, Papa."

"Maybe not now, but in a few years—"

She held up her hands, palms outward. "Stop. You have to stop planning my life for me. Did you ever think it might not be my destiny to be married, Papa?"

"Marriage is in every Mancini's destiny," he proclaimed.

"Maybe, but that doesn't mean I don't need a job."

"A job is fine, but family must come first. I'm afraid you're going to discover this job has kept you from finding what really matters in life."

Kika sighed. "Papa, you're the one who taught me to reach for the stars. Don't you want me to succeed?"

"Of course I do, but I can't pretend I'm happy with this business you're running—the people you meet, the hours you have to keep. I don't trust these show-biz types."

"I can handle them."

He harrumphed. "How are you going to meet a real man to settle down with when all you're ever surrounded by are ones made up of plastic parts?" He gestured wildly with his hands.

Kika knew it would do no good to tell her father that she wasn't looking for a man, that she was looking for a rewarding career. To him, the career a woman strived to achieve was that of wife and mother. All three of her brothers had given him grandchildren. Now she was expected to follow in their tracks.

Unfortunately, her tracks led to the fast lane. She wanted to be the best casting director in the Midwest, and she was well on her way to earning that reputation. The Fancy contract was proof. She looped her arm through her father's and smiled up at him affectionately.

"Papa, you don't need to worry about me falling for an actor or a model. When I fall in love, it will be with someone who is genuine and down-to-earth—like you. Now we'd better get going or I'll miss my plane."

He sighed. "I wish you weren't traveling alone. Promise me you'll be careful."

"I promise."

"And watch out for the men. You're a beautiful young woman, Kika. Any father in my position would worry."

As much as Kika wanted to be impatient with her overprotective parent, she found it rather endearing the way he honestly believed that she was irresistible to men.

"I'm going to Tyler, Wisconsin, not New York City. And I'm going in search of a baby, not a man."

But it was a man who caught Kika's eye at the Milwaukee airport. As she dragged her wheeled suitcase through the terminal, she spotted him in a crush of people deplaning at one of the gates.

He was tall with short dark hair, deepset eyes and a wholesomeness that made Kika think she could cast him in a dozen parts as the "guy who gets the girl." He looked familiar, but it was only when he smiled at one of the flight attendants that Kika recognized him from T.J.'s Playmates video.

A glance at the reservation desk told her the plane had just arrived from Los Angeles. The possibility that he was an actor and not a day-care father increased. He certainly had the good looks to be one of the Hollywood crowd. Could he be on his way to Tyler, just as she was?

He looked up and their eyes connected for the briefest of moments. Frannie was right; he was a hunk. Automatically, Kika's lips parted in a grin. He looked away, but not before she had noticed a flicker of interest. She continued on her way, dragging her suitcase behind her.

When she arrived at the rental-car counter, there was a line of people waiting to be served. Tired, Kika set her briefcase on the floor beside her suitcase. As she dug through her wallet for her credit card, she sensed someone come up behind her.

A quick glance told her it was the man from T.J.'s video. He was even better-looking up close than he had been from a distance. Automatically, Kika's eyes were drawn to his left hand. There was no wedding ring.

Of course, she knew that didn't mean he wasn't married, but at least there wasn't an obvious Keep Off sign. Unashamedly and with a professional eye, she looked him over, taking in the details she hadn't had time to notice at the gate—his short, straight nose, the little mole right beneath his chin, the dark hairs on the back of his hands. He was a fine specimen of manhood—in the professional sense, of course. It wouldn't surprise her if he were an actor.

And he smelled good. It was an unfamiliar fragrance. In her line of business, she had interviewed many men, most of them wearing designer colognes, but this one she didn't recognize.

Always thinking of work, she made a mental inventory of the clients she thought might be interested in the "guy who gets the girl" look. She debated whether she should give him her business card with the suggestion that he contact her. She could find him plenty of work. Before she said a word, however, he spoke to her.

"If you're not careful, you might lose something," he stated in a voice that was as impersonal and polite as a taxicab driver's.

Kika glanced down to see that her suitcase had come partially unzipped and a pair of red bikini briefs threatened to fall out. With an embarrassed grin, she bent down and pulled the zipper shut around the underwear. "Thanks." With the ease of someone who had years of experience flirting with men, she allowed her gaze to linger on him just a bit longer than was necessary, a hint of her smile remaining.

He nodded and glanced at his wristwatch, clearly indicating he had no interest in any further conversation.

His reaction didn't surprise Kika. She chalked it up to the typical arrogance she encountered whenever she worked with extremely good-looking men.

This fellow obviously didn't want to be bothered. Which was fine, since she really had no reason to flirt with him anyway. All she knew about him was that he had been in a children's video. She was relieved when the clerk at the desk said, "Next."

Kika moved to the counter, all the time aware of the man behind her. As she waited for her rental agreement to be processed, he, too, stepped up to the counter just a few feet away from her. While he completed his transaction, Kika studied his profile and found her muscles tensing involuntarily. It was a physical reaction, pure and simple.

She was relieved when the clerk returned with keys to a Chevy Corsica and directions to the parking lot. As Kika expected, the passenger from L.A. was right behind her when she stepped outside.

Watch out for the men. Her father's warning played in her memory. She walked with confidence across the pavement. It was silly to allow her father's overprotectiveness to make her uneasy. The man whose footsteps echoed hers wasn't interested in her at all. That was why she jumped when he called out to her. "Wait!"

When she turned, he handed her the compact umbrella that usually fit in the side of her carry-on bag. "You dropped this. You'll probably need it. It looks like rain." He pointed to the sky, where jagged lightning broke the summer darkness.

"Thank you. Again." She flashed him a grateful grin.

This time there was an answering smile on his face. It made dimples appear and caused Kika's insides to do a funky little dance.

"Do you know what a white Corsica looks like?" she asked.

"No, but I have a blue one." He looked out across the rows of rental cars and pointed to his right. "I think they're over there."

Thunder rumbled in the distance as they walked toward the cars prompting Kika to say, "I hope it's not going to storm before I reach my hotel."

"Where are you staying?"

Kika knew better than to answer that one. "At a bed-and-breakfast. What about you?"

"I'm stuck with my mother-in-law."

Oh, no, he's married! "Lucky you," she said with a forced grin. Curious, she couldn't resist asking, "You here on business?"

He nodded. "I'm starting a new job. What about you?"

"Oh, business," she answered. "Have you worked in Milwaukee before?"

"No, I'm from L.A."

They had reached the rental cars. Without another word, she located the white Corsica and stuck a key in the trunk. As she tossed her overnight bag inside, he opened the car next to hers.

After slamming the trunk, she automatically glanced in his direction. He was pulling a jacket out of his suitcase. Before he closed the leather bag, however, Kika noticed he had a pair of handcuffs and a blindfold. She quickly looked away.

Married, an actor and kinky. The guy had three strikes against him. Relieved that he hadn't responded to her flirting, she climbed into her rental car.

By the time she had started the engine and become familiar with the instrument panel, the lightning was closer. Within seconds, rain pelted the windows so that when Kika glanced at the man in the car next to hers, she saw nothing but a blur.

As she drove out of the parking lot she noticed the blue Corsica was right behind her. When she turned onto the freeway, it followed. She slowed, hoping he would pass her, but he remained directly behind her.

When the rain became so heavy that she could barely see the highway lines, Kika pulled over to the side of the road. The blue Corsica drove past and she breathed a sigh of relief.

While she waited for the rain to subside, she studied the map the clerk at the car-rental agency had given her. The road she was to take was highlighted in yellow.

It was after ten when she turned down Main Street in Tyler, but the town looked as if it were three a.m. In the warm glow of street lamps there wasn't a soul in sight. Wendy had arranged for her to spend the night at a bed-and-breakfast called Granny Rose's. Kika hoped Granny Rose was still awake, for it was obvious that most of Tyler was asleep.

The small, dainty woman who answered the door of the big old Victorian house was not old nor was she a granny, and she was definitely wide-awake. Her thickly lashed, luminous blue eyes gazed at Kika with a curious gleam.

"You must be Ms. Mancini," she said, looking her over with a friendly eye. "I'm Susannah Santori. Come in."

Kika stepped inside the beautifully decorated home. "This is lovely," she said, taking in the Victorian interior.

"Thank you. It was my grandmother's house. My husband, Joe, did all the renovations." She reached for a switch that sent a flood of light illuminating a small study off the front hallway. "You'll have to pardon the darkness but our guests usually arrive earlier in the evening."

"I'm sorry, I hope it's not a problem," Kika said apologetically.

"Oh, not at all. I'm a night owl myself." She led Kika over to a rolltop desk, where she gestured for her to take a seat. "If you would fill out the registration form, I'll get the key to your room and you can settle in."

Kika furnished the necessary information on the card, then handed it back to Susannah, who scanned it and said, "Mancini's an Italian name."

"Yes. I fool people with my blond hair. Most people expect Italians to be brunette."

"But you have dark eyes." She tucked the registration into an index-card file. "And you have that look about you."

"What look is that?"

She shrugged. "I don't know. My husband, Joe, has it, too. You look so full of life."

Kika smiled. "I'll take that as a compliment."

"Oh, it is." She stood and motioned for Kika to follow. "I'll show you where everything is." She gave her a brief tour of the dining and sitting rooms before leading her up the staircase. "Is this your first visit to Tyler?" she asked.

"Yes. I didn't even know there was a Tyler, Wisconsin, until I saw one of the day-care-center videos."

"Oh. Is that why you're here? Because of the videos?"

"I have an appointment with a woman named Glenna McRoberts. I believe she works at the TylerTots Community Day Care?"

"She sure does. Glenna's a great gal. Talented and very smart." They entered a room that was cornflower-blue and white, with a large four-poster bed and a homemade quilt.

"Then you know her?"

"Umm-hmm." Susannah set Kika's suitcase on a luggage stand at the end of the bed. "The success of the videos has had everyone talking. It's been fun for the kids.''

''I have an appointment with Glenna tomorrow morning at the day-care center. Is that far from here?''

''Oh, no. It's really close. Just go two blocks down Morgan and take a left. You can't miss it. It's in the basement of Sarah's church.''

Seeing Kika's puzzled look, she added, ''That's the Tyler Fellowship. Sarah Kenton's the minister.''

The thought of a woman minister in a town the size of Tyler appealed to Kika. ''Then I'll be able to walk?''

''Sure. If you tell me what time your appointment is, I'll make sure you get breakfast before you go.''

''I'm supposed to be there at nine.''

''Perfect. We usually serve between seven-thirty and eight.'' Susannah walked over to the nightstand beside the bed and lifted a piece of paper. ''Here's the menu choices. If you want to look at it and then slip it under the door, everything will be ready when you are.''

''Great.''

''And there's a library down the hall on your left. It's the only room with an open door. You can't miss it.'' She turned back the bed and fluffed the pillows. ''Your secretary said you were only staying the one night, right?''

Kika nodded.

''If that changes, just let me know.'' She walked over to the French doors, which opened onto a small balcony. ''Oh, good, the rain has stopped.''

''Is it always this quiet?'' Kika asked as she followed the innkeeper outside.

"Most of the time."

"Quite different from the city," Kika remarked.

"I know. It took me a while to get used to the absence of noise when I first moved back."

"Did you grow up here?"

"Umm-hmm, but I worked for a while in Milwaukee. I had my own television show called 'Oh, Susannah!' I demonstrated cooking tips, gave household hints, interviewed celebrities. It was a fun program."

"Why did you leave?"

"I fell in love." She smiled reflectively. "Although to be perfectly honest, I had become a bit restless in Milwaukee. I guess it just took the right circumstances to show me that."

Kika understood what she meant. There were times when restlessness had her questioning the direction of her own life. "Do you miss your television career?"

The woman pondered the question for a moment before saying, "You know, I really don't. I enjoy small-town living, and the people you meet in the television world can be so..." She paused, searching for the right word.

"Superficial?" Kika supplied.

She chuckled. "Come to think of it, that's a pretty good word to describe my old boss. How did you know?"

"Because I work in television. I have a casting agency for TV and film."

Suzannah's delicate jaw fell. "It's a small world, isn't it? I wouldn't expect to find a casting agent visiting Tyler. Is that why you're here to see Glenna? Because of your work?"

"It's for professional reasons, yes," Kika answered, trying not to say too much about her visit until after she had talked to the producer of the videos. She was grateful Susannah Santori didn't press her for information.

"This balcony's a great spot to relax, but be careful," the innkeeper warned, running her fingers across the back of a lawn chair. "Everything's still wet from the storm that passed through."

Kika nodded, then followed Susannah back inside. She expected the former television star to ask her more about her work, but she didn't. She just said, "If there's anything at all you need, just pick up the phone and press zero. I'll be right downstairs."

It was an exhausted Kika who slid between the cool cotton sheets shortly thereafter. Every night before she fell asleep she mentally prepared for the next day. As she lay in the strange bedroom she tried to think about the little redheaded girl in the video, but all she could see was a tall, dark, handsome man, whose cheeks dimpled when he smiled and who carried handcuffs and a blindfold in his suitcase.

"YIPPEE. DAD'S HERE!"

Nick awoke to the sound of feet trampling across the wooden floor, and before he could even sit up, two bodies landed on his.

"Grandma wouldn't let us wait up for you last night," Patrick said, straddling Nick's midsection.

"That's cuz she wanted to watch Letterman and she was worried we'd hear some swear words," Zachary told him, sitting cross-legged so that his toes were in Nick's face.

Nick propped a couple of pillows behind his neck and shifted Patrick so that he could get a better perspective. "I missed you guys."

"We missed you, too, Dad," they said in unison, practically smothering him with hugs and kisses.

"Grandma's strict," Zachary announced in a disapproving tone.

"She's just doing what she thinks is best." Nick defended his mother-in-law, although personally he agreed with the boys. From his phone conversations with Annabelle he knew that she was firm with her grandchildren.

"Yeah, she won't let us play Nintendo cuz she thinks it's going to wreck her TV," Zachary complained.

"And we have to do Legos on the floor because she says they'll scratch her table," Patrick added.

Nick raised a finger to his lips and quieted them. "We're going to have our own house soon and then you can go back to doing things the way you've always done them. But while you're at Grandma's, you need to respect her rules."

"Aww, Dad," they groaned in chorus.

"Now tell me all the good stuff that's happened while I've been gone."

They were in the middle of explanations when Annabelle's loud voice echoed from the hallway. "Melody would like to come in. Is it safe?"

Safe? Nick wondered what his mother-in-law thought could be dangerous about his daughter coming into his bedroom. Did she think he slept in the nude?

"It's fine, Annabelle. The boys and I are just catching up."

Annabelle poked her head around the door frame gingerly, before entering. When she saw that the three of them were presentable, she pulled Melody into the room.

"Go see your daddy," she told her granddaughter in a soft voice Nick had never heard her use before.

Melody's lower lip was pushed out in an expression Nick remembered well. It had been nearly a month since he had seen his daughter, yet very little had changed, except her red curls drooped a little closer to her shoulders.

"Go on, dear," Annabelle urged, but Melody hung back, her pointer finger pushed against her tiny mouth. "Go on, Melody, give your daddy a hug," Annabelle repeated more forcefully, but Melody refused to move.

"I don't think she likes Grandma," Zachary said in a whisper only his father could hear.

Nick could only hope that wasn't true. He had come to Tyler so that Annabelle could be a positive influence on his daughter. He knew from longtime experience that his mother-in-law could be intimidating. In the past few weeks had she been gruff with his children?

"Hello, Melody," he said tenderly, giving his daughter a smile.

She didn't respond, only continued to suck on her finger and pout. Finally, Annabelle picked her up and started to carry her over to the bed. Melody began to kick and holler.

"She's being ornery again," Patrick announced. Her grandmother paid no attention.

Nick did. "It's all right, Annabelle. I'm sure Melody will come get her hug when she's ready."

Reluctantly, Annabelle set the squirming toddler down. Melody ran back to the door and hid her face on her chubby little arm.

Nick wanted to rush over and scoop her up in his arms and hug her tightly, but he was afraid she'd run away from him, and that was something he couldn't bear. Ever since the day he had brought her home without her mother, it was as if she could sense his pain. He had done everything he could not to see Beth in Melody's angelic little face, yet not once when he looked at her was he not reminded of his wife.

He knew it was ridiculous to think that a twenty-two-month-old child could sense what a troubled heart her father had. He didn't want Beth to be between them. It wasn't his daughter's fault that his wife had died. If blame was to be placed, it would be on his own shoulders. He was the one who had insisted they have a third child. Melody hadn't asked to be born. Yet it was as if his daughter knew her mother was gone because she was here.

It was something he hadn't talked about with Annabelle. How could he? It was too horrible to say aloud. He had hoped that if he ignored the feelings of guilt and the what-might-have-beens, the strain in his relationship with his daughter would disappear.

It hadn't, and now he had come to Tyler, Beth's hometown, to be with Beth's mother and her sister in hopes they would help right the wrong he was doing his daughter. For he had to be doing something wrong with her. Why else wouldn't she talk? And why didn't she wrap her arms around him and kiss and hug him like the boys did?

"Hey, Dad! Did you get the magic stuff?" Zachary asked, interrupting his father's musings.

"Yup. It's in my suitcase. There's a blindfold, a pair of handcuffs and the book of magic tricks. We'll look at them after we've had breakfast."

That had the boys bouncing out of bed and racing to get dressed. As soon as they were gone, he noticed that Melody still stood outside his door. Waiting.

Pulling his bathrobe over his pajamas, Nick poked his head around the doorjamb and asked, "Want a piggyback ride downstairs?"

She nodded shyly. Nick bent down and let her climb up onto his back. She was warm and soft against him, causing his heart to flutter with mixed emotions. As he galloped down the stairs, she giggled, her chubby little fists clinging to his neck. Before he deposited her in her high chair, he gave her a hug and kissed her on the cheek.

"I missed you, Melody."

She didn't utter a sound, but clung to his neck for dear life, as if she thought he'd drop her. Finally Annabelle's imposing voice had her loosening her grip.

"The children better eat or else they're going to be late."

While Annabelle was at work, Melody spent the day at TylerTots. Patrick and Zachary were enrolled in a summer program at the elementary school called Adventure Club.

Nick settled Melody in the high chair. "They don't have to go this morning. I'll take care of them."

"What about your appointment with the real-estate agent?"

"It's not until this afternoon. I'll drop them off on my way."

Annabelle frowned. "What about their lunch?"

"I can fix them something," Nick assured her.

Skepticism crinkled his mother-in-law's face. "I can come home on my lunch break if you want me to."

"No. You have lunch with your friends as usual. We'll be fine here, won't we, Melody?" He gave his daughter a wink. She didn't respond. When Annabelle started dishing up bowls of oatmeal, he nudged her aside, saying, "Here, let me do that. You go to work."

Annabelle looked as if she wanted to protest, but just then the boys came racing into the kitchen with their arms spread wide, making airplane sounds. When Zachary saw what his father was spooning into the breakfast bowls, he let out a groan. "Oh, no! Not oatmeal again!"

Patrick continued to race around the room, one arm still outstretched. With his other hand he pinched his nose, causing his "Yuck! Yuck! Yuck!" to have a nasal sound.

"Boys!" Nick's reprimand silenced both of them. To Annabelle he said, "We'll be all right."

The look on her face said she didn't believe him, but she left just the same.

As soon as the back door had slammed shut, Nick dumped the oatmeal in the garbage and pulled out the frying pan. "How does French toast sound?" he asked.

KIKA LOOKED at her watch and saw that it was only six-thirty. What had woken her? Maybe it was the absence of sound. In Minneapolis she went to sleep and awoke to the cacophony of traffic speeding down the interstate near her apartment complex. This morning she heard nothing, not even the hum of the air conditioner.

She climbed out of bed and padded over to the French doors leading to the tiny balcony. She pushed on the brass handle and gasped in delight at the beautiful sight that greeted her. The early-morning sun left a hazy, yellow glow on the green lawns of Tyler, the dew sparkling like diamonds.

There was a small coffeepot in the room, and Kika brewed a cup of French vanilla. Then she did something she rarely did at home—she sat outside in the morning quiet and watched the small town come awake.

As she did so, she visualized what she wanted to happen later that morning. She would go to the TylerTots center, speak with Glenna McRoberts and learn the name of the little redhead in the video, then contact the parents of the child. It was a doable job, one she could accomplish with the right approach. And there was no doubt in her mind that she had the right approach.

After a delicious breakfast, during which Susannah Santori demonstrated why she had been such a popular TV personality, fixing an array of dishes worthy of a four-star restaurant in the city, Kika slipped into a sleeveless denim vest and a long floral skirt. Wearing a pair of black boots that laced up the front, she walked the three blocks to the Tyler Fellowship Sanctuary. At exactly nine o'clock, she presented herself at TylerTots Community Day Care.

Angela Murphy, the day-care center's director, greeted her with a smile and introduced her to Glenna McRoberts, who Kika learned was a part-time preschool teacher. Flattered by Kika's praise for her ingenuity, Glenna readily answered all her questions regarding production of the Playmates video. Then she gave Kika a tour of the day-care facility and introduced her to the other staff members, including Daphne Sullivan, a tall, willowy blonde who had a two-year-old enrolled at TylerTots.

All of the staff were welcoming, with the exception of Daphne. Kika wasn't sure if it was personal or if the woman simply didn't approve of Kika's reasons for being there.

Throughout the tour Kika had looked for the little redhead, but didn't see her. When it was over, she broached the subject with Glenna. "There was a toddler in one of your videos," she said. "She had red hair, didn't play with the others but stood off in a corner."

"Oh, you must mean Melody."

Melody. Even though the child had appeared sullen, Kika thought the name somehow suited her. "Is she still here?"

"Well, yes, she is. Only today she's not coming in until this afternoon."

"How old is she?"

"Almost two. Is she one of the children you saw on the video who you think might work in one of your commercials?"

"There's a possibility she could be."

Glenna sighed. "Oh, isn't it unfortunate that she's not here."

"I'd like to meet her, but my flight is at one-thirty." Kika knew she needed an hour to drive back to Milwaukee, plus time to return the rental car and check in at the airlines. If she was going to see this Melody, it would have to be before noon. "Could you give me her parents' address and phone number?"

"Oh, I'm sorry, Ms. Mancini. That would be against the center's policy—unless, of course, we had her parents' permission."

Kika understood the need for confidentiality. "Maybe you could give them a call and see if it's all right? I wouldn't ask except this really is a wonderful opportunity for little Melody."

Glenna hesitated only briefly, then excused herself. Kika watched her go into the office and use the telephone. It wasn't long before she returned, an apologetic look on her face.

"I'm sorry, Ms. Mancini. There was no answer. If you'd like to leave your name and number, I'd be happy to pass it on."

Kika glanced at her watch. "I'll tell you what. How about if I make a couple of phone calls and come back this afternoon?"

"But I thought you were leaving this morning."

"That's why I need to make the phone calls. If I can catch a flight later, I'd like to spend the day here at TylerTots... if that's all right with you? I'd like to observe the children at play."

"I'll have to check with Angela, but I'm sure she won't object." Glenna gave her a warm smile and excused herself. Kika returned the smile, thinking that one way or another, she was going to see Melody. If the baby wasn't going to be in until the afternoon, then Kika would rearrange her schedule to make sure she was there in the afternoon. She hadn't come this far for nothing.

Within minutes, Glenna returned. "Angela says you're welcome to stay."

"Thank you. I'll be sure to come right back."

CHAPTER THREE

INSTEAD OF HIRING a baby-sitter to stay with his children while he was at work, Nick had taken his mother-in-law's recommendation that he enroll the boys in Adventure Club and leave Melody at TylerTots day care. Annabelle had assured him that his daughter would like going to the bright, cheerful center and that it would be a good opportunity for her to socialize with other children her age.

When he parked his car in front of the Tyler Fellowship Sanctuary and Melody began to fuss, however, he began to question his mother-in-law's advice. From the expression on his daughter's face, he could see she didn't want to go inside.

"Mr. Miller, it's good to see you again," Angela Murphy said in greeting when he carried Melody in. "Hi, Melody." She gave the toddler a warm smile.

Nick attempted to set his daughter down, but she clung to his shirt collar and buried her face in his neck.

Angela opened her arms. "Come, Melody. Let's go see what we can find to do."

Her answer was a grunt, which Nick knew meant no. When Angela attempted to take her from her father's arms, she stiffened. According to Annabelle, Melody hadn't objected to being left at the day-care center. If that were the case, Nick wondered why was she clinging to him for dear life.

"I'll tell you what. It's almost snack time. Maybe your daddy would like to eat with us?" Angela spoke to Melody, but looked at Nick.

"Would it be all right?" he asked, reluctant to pry his daughter's fingers from his shirt.

"Of course. We have one other guest as well. Actually, it's someone who's been waiting to speak to you. A Ms. Mancini. She's in the office."

The director pointed to a room that had Plexiglas on the upper half of its walls. Sitting with her back to them was a woman with long blond hair.

Nick walked toward the office. As he drew closer, he saw that the woman was on the phone. Unintentionally, he overheard her end of the conversation.

"Oh, my God, Lucy. It's awful. There are babies everywhere!"

There was distress in the vaguely familiar voice. Nick paused outside the door, wondering what kind of woman came to a day-care center and complained about children.

"I don't have much choice." Silence. "Uh-uh." Silence. "I know." Silence. "You're right. I can do this." She paused again, then said, "But this is it. No more kids. I just don't want to be around them."

She lowered her voice, then hung up, and Nick decided it was time to make his presence known. He rapped on the Plexiglas and received a bit of a jolt when Ms. Mancini turned around. Staring at him was the woman he had seen at the airport last night.

She had the most gorgeous shade of blond hair, yet her skin wasn't fair, but a honey gold, and her eyes were dark. Last night her voluptuous figure had been hidden by a raincoat, but today he could see every curve and angle, and the vision was spectacular. Wearing a vest that fit her bosom like a glove and earrings that chimed when she moved her head, she looked totally out of place in a day-care center.

At the airport he had been too tired to respond to her flirting. Today his blood surged through his body at the sight of her gazing at him with interest. It had been a long, long time since he had had the urge to respond to that interest.

"So we meet again," she said amiably as Nick stepped inside the office. This time the flirtatious tone was noticeably absent. She stood up, causing the slit in her long skirt to split and reveal a length of golden leg. "I'm Kika Mancini," she said, offering her hand to Nick.

He shifted Melody to his left side, freeing his right hand so that he could shake it. "Nick Miller," he said, trying not to notice the cleavage revealed by her vest.

"And this must be Melody," Kika said, her eyes perusing the toddler in a very thorough manner.

"Melody, can you say hello to Kika?" Nick asked.

She lifted her head from her father's neck to shyly peek at Kika, but that was all.

"She's lovely," Kika said, her eyes meeting Nick's.

"Thank you." Stunned by Kika's own beauty, he nearly forgot to ask the questions that only seconds ago had been burning his mind: why was she waiting for him and how did she know Melody's name?

As if she could read his mind, she said, "I recognize Melody from Glenna's Playmates video. She said it was shot the day you enrolled Melody."

"Ah." He had completely forgotten about the waiver he had signed giving his permission for his daughter to be on the film.

"It's because of Glenna's video that I'm here."

Puzzled, he wanted to ask her what she meant. He didn't. He was having a difficult time forming any questions at all. He was distracted by the gentle swell of flesh at the neckline of her vest. At least his hormones were.

Finally, he managed to say, "I understand you've been waiting to see me."

"Yes, you and Melody." Again the little girl turned her head away shyly.

"Why?"

"Maybe we should sit down and I'll explain?" Kika ushered him out of the office, past beanbag chairs and cots to one of the long, low tables against the wall.

Again Nick tried to pry Melody from his neck and put her on a chair beside him, but she refused to budge. To say he felt ridiculous sitting on a miniature chair was an understatement. He debated whether he should return to a standing position, but wasn't sure he would be able to get back up without embarrassing himself even further—not with Melody clinging to him.

He couldn't tell if the sparkle in Kika's eye was humor or interest.

"Mr. Miller, have you ever heard of Fancy Furniture?"

"Yes, hasn't everyone?"

"It's an old, established name with a reputation for quality," Kika said smoothly. "My grandmother has one of those big oak pedestal tables with the hand-carved chairs. You know, come to think of it, I'm staying at Granny Rose's Bed-and-Breakfast and I'm pretty sure the bedroom set in the room I'm in is a Fancy, too.''

"I wouldn't know. I haven't been to Granny Rose's.''

She flashed him a little smile that he found extremely attractive, then said, ''Do you have any Fancy furniture yourself?''

If he had, it had all been sold. He was making a fresh start. Besides, the house he would be moving into the first of the month came completely furnished.

"I don't believe I do,'' he answered.

"Me neither.''

"I think my grandmother had a few pieces,'' he told her, wanting to be amenable.

"Yes, well, our grandmothers knew what quality furniture was. And that's my point. Fancy has a wonderful reputation with the older segment of the population, but until recently, they haven't been known for appealing to the younger generation. Young married couples with children usually inherit their Fancy pieces, rather than purchase them themselves. That's why Fancy has decided to develop a whole new line of products specifically for couples in their twenties and thirties. Children's furniture!'' Kika's hands moved as smoothly as a dancer's. ''You know, youth beds, cribs, wardrobes, desks, bunk beds—that sort of stuff.''

"And you want me to buy some of this new furniture?'' he asked, thinking he should feel turned off by her sales pitch, but unable to muster any annoyance with the unwanted solicitation. Probably because she was so enthusiastic as she talked about the product. He liked the way her hands moved when she spoke.

"Oh, no. I'm not selling Fancy furniture—well, not in the literal sense, anyway." She had a wonderful little laugh that caused his insides to tingle.

"So what's your 'un-literal' sense?" he asked with a wink. Maybe he hadn't lost his touch, after all, he thought as her eyes met his and he saw a sparkle of interest.

"I do work for Horace Fancy."

"The president of Fancy Furniture?"

"Umm-hmm. I should explain." She had a way of looking at him that made him feel as if she were a close friend. "To launch this new line of children's products, Fancy is going to have a tremendous advertising campaign that will air nationally."

"And you're part of that advertising campaign?"

"It's why I'm here in Tyler. I'm looking for the right person to help make Fancy a well-known name in every family—not just our grandmothers'."

"And how do you plan to do that, Ms. Mancini?" Nick asked.

"Oh, please. Call me Kika."

"Very well, Kika. What does Fancy's advertising campaign have to do with my daughter? Are you looking for a consumer test market or something?" He leaned closer to her, giving her his undivided attention.

"It's the 'or something,'" she said with a sly grin. She reached inside her briefcase and extracted a business card. "I'm a casting director, Mr. Miller, and I've been hired to find that one very special toddler who can win the hearts of mothers and fathers all across the country, a baby who will become such a well-known TV personality that the minute someone sees her picture they'll think of Fancy furniture.''

Nick could only stare in disbelief. This woman couldn't possibly think Melody was that baby? Yet he could see by the way she was eyeing his daughter that was exactly what she thought.

"The reason I've come to Tyler is because I think I might find that baby here. Of course, I won't know for sure until I've conducted an audition, but judging by what I saw in Glenna's video, I'm very optimistic.''

With a furrowed brow, Nick glanced at the neon-pink business card. Ms. Kika Mancini was in show business. If the fact that she didn't like children hadn't been enough to put the brakes on his hormones, her occupation should be.

He had left California to get away from people like Kika, people who thought that having a pretty face and getting in front of a camera were all that mattered in life. Never would he have imagined that Hollywood would follow him to Tyler, Wisconsin.

"It's really a wonderful opportunity for any child, Mr. Miller,'' she continued. "Fancy Furniture commercials will air frequently, which means the residuals from the television spot alone will be quite lucrative. Besides TV there will also be a print campaign. Your daughter could earn enough from this one booking to make a nice college nest egg.''

Nick continued to stare at Kika in disbelief. She was carrying on as if she had just offered him the chance of a lifetime. Again, he found himself at a loss for words.

"All you have to do, Mr. Miller, is bring Melody to Minneapolis for an audition. We can make it whenever it's convenient for you. Of course, the sooner the better." She flashed him another of her dazzling smiles, and Nick felt a surge of adrenaline.

"So what do you say? What date would be good for you to bring Melody for a screen test?" She flung open an appointment book and looked at it thoughtfully. "Next week is the Fourth of July, which means it'll be hard to get a crew together." She flipped another page and wrinkled her nose. "Is there any possibility you could come to Minneapolis the following week?" She looked at him hopefully.

"No."

"What about the second week then?"

"No."

"The third?"

"No. You can close your appointment book, Ms. Mancini. I'm not bringing my daughter to any audition," he stated firmly.

The sparkle in her eyes disappeared. "If you'd like some time to think this over, I understand, Mr. Miller."

"I don't need any time."

Her lips tightened as she searched for the right words. "This is a once-in-a-lifetime opportunity for any child."

"Melody isn't 'any' child, Ms. Mancini. She's my daughter and I don't want her innocence exploited."

Kika rushed to the defense. "I understand your concerns. You wouldn't be a good parent if you didn't question the circumstances. But I can assure you that there are very strict child-labor laws that protect children. The welfare of the child is always the primary concern in situations like this. Melody would be treated with exceptionally good care," she said with a sincerity that would have sold almost any man. But Nick Miller was not any man.

"She's not going to be part of any TV commercial," he declared unemotionally.

He could see by the gleam in Kika's eye that she was not about to give up. "Mr. Miller, do you realize that thousands, no probably hundreds of thousands of parents would love to have an opportunity like this for their child?"

"Then you shouldn't have any problem finding Fancy's Baby, should you?" he retorted.

While they had been talking, Melody had lifted her head from her father's shoulder and was staring at Kika. In fact, the normally shy toddler was rather enchanted by the woman with the animated facial expressions and hand gestures.

Kika closed her datebook and looked him squarely in the eyes. "Maybe before you make any decisions you should talk it over with your wife. If you like, I'd be happy to speak to her, answer any questions she has."

"That won't be necessary. I'm a single parent, Ms. Mancini," he said soberly. "I make all of the decisions regarding Melody."

"I see." She regarded him pensively, then said, "Mr. Miller, may I ask what you do for a living?"

"I'm a mechanical engineer," he answered.

One eyebrow lifted delicately. "I see. Then you've had no experience with AFTRA, the actors' union."

"No, nor do I intend to," he assured her.

At that point Angela came over carrying a tray of fruit cups. "You will stay and have snack time with us, won't you, Kika?"

"Actually, I should be going so that I can catch my plane back to Minneapolis." She closed her briefcase with a snap and slung her purse strap over her shoulder.

To Nick's dismay, Melody watched in fascination.

"You are such a cutie," Kika said to the toddler, reaching out to touch her cheek tenderly.

Nick expected his daughter to shy away in fright, but to his surprise, she smiled at the casting director.

"I hope you'll think about what I said, Mr. Miller." She batted her long lashes in a soft plea that Nick assumed she often used to get her own way. He mentally shook his head. People in the entertainment industry would do anything to get ahead.

"Melody is not for sale," he told her, ignoring the temptation to respond to that plea.

She sighed. "This isn't a question of selling your daughter. It's an investment for her future." She extended her hand to Nick. "You have my card. Please don't hesitate to call if you have any questions at all."

Reluctantly, he shook her hand and felt her warmth penetrate his skin. He liked the feel of her hand in his. As she walked toward the exit, he decided it wasn't the only thing he liked about Kika Mancini.

Nick watched as she exchanged words with Angela before leaving. He had a feeling she'd be back. She had that look of determination in her eye.

Part of him wasn't sorry.

"I'M GOING TO DO a talent search in Tyler, Wisconsin." Kika told her aunt Lucy the following morning.

At forty-six, Lucia Vescio looked young enough to be mistaken for Kika's sister. She had the same golden-blond hair, only Lucy tamed hers with a scarf, pulling it straight back and securing it at her neck. As a modeling agent, she had launched the careers of many young men and women, earning the respect of her peers. To Kika, she was like a second mother, someone her niece could turn to whenever she needed sound advice.

"You really think that you'll be able to find the Fancy baby in a small town of ten thousand?" Lucy asked as she perched on the corner of Kika's desk.

"I have a hunch on this one," Kika replied, tossing a wad of paper into the wastebasket.

"Then you'd better do it. Your hunches are usually right on. So when is all this going to happen?"

"I'm going to set it up for the second week in July. I thought I'd spend the Fourth in Tyler and get to know some of the people, see what I can find out about the babies in the area." She leaned back in her chair reflectively. "You know, I should have thought of this sooner. What better place to find a fresh face than in a small town?"

Lucy pinned her with her gaze. "Are you sure you're going to be all right with this one? Yesterday you called to tell me you were having trouble with the whole project."

"The trouble's no different than I've had with every job that's involved babies. Every time I see a little girl I can't help but wonder what my own daughter would have looked like had she lived...." Her voice faded with emotion.

Lucy moved around the desk until she stood in front of her. "Kika, you have to let go of the past. How long are you going to punish yourself for this?"

"How long am I going to believe I deserve to be punished?"

Lucy took her niece's hands in hers. "Listen to me. Babies die during labor even when mothers do everything right. That's a fact of life."

"Maybe I didn't do everything right."

"You don't believe all that junk about Sophie Carzone losing her baby because it was illegitimate? Kika, God doesn't punish anyone for conceiving a child outside of marriage."

"You're right," she stated smoothly.

"Yes, I am, and you're a smart woman. You know better than to believe the old wives' tales of your grandmother's cronies."

Intellectually, Kika did. So why did that tiny kernel of guilt refuse to disappear? "It doesn't matter."

"Yes, it does if it interferes with your work. Would you like me to come with you to Tyler?"

She shook her head. "You have too much work to do. Besides, I think I can take care of everything in a week."

"You're convinced you can find Fancy's Baby in Tyler?"

"I'm hoping I already have." Kika told her aunt about Melody Miller and her father's lack of interest in the project.

"You think you can change his mind?"

"I think it's worth a shot." As she talked about her work, the sadness disappeared from her eyes, replaced by an enthusiasm that brought color back to her cheeks.

"We'll distribute flyers, run an ad in the newspaper—the *Tyler Citizen*—and do some radio spots. We need to get the word out that we're coming to town to find a baby.''

"This is going to cost a few extra bucks. I'm surprised Fancy went along with it.''

"He's the one demanding we get a toddler who looks like the little girl next door. What better place to look than in small-town America?''

"I think it's a great idea. I'm just worried about you. Being so far away from home and around all those babies.''

The concern in her aunt's eyes touched Kika deeply. "I have a good feeling on this one.''

"Well, I want you to know you can call me if you need me.''

Kika give her a hug. "Thanks.''

Later that evening, Kika sat with notepad in hand, watching the Video Playmates series. However, very few words appeared on the paper, for she kept playing one segment of the tape over and over—the part where Nick Miller appeared.

"So he's not an actor, after all,'' she mumbled to herself. "Nor is he married. But there is still the problem of the handcuffs.''

"WE BROUGHT FOOD.''

Nick looked up from the pile of boxes to find his sister-in-law, Cece Baron, standing in the doorway of the kitchen, a pan of brownies in her hands. Standing beside her were her three-year-old twins, Annie and Belle. One held a package of hot dog buns, the other a stack of paper plates. Cece's husband, Jeff, carried a small cooler.

"It looks like you could use a couple of extra hands," Jeff commented as he stepped around boxes to get near the table.

"This is the stuff my mother called odds and ends," Nick explained. "She said she'd pack it up for us and send it on ahead. I thought with all the furniture being sold, there'd be hardly anything left. I was wrong."

"Speaking of mothers, where's mine?" Cece asked, setting the brownies on the counter. "I thought she was going to help."

"She's still packing up the stuff the kids left at her house, then she'll be over," Nick told her.

Cece took the paper plates and hot dog buns from her daughters' hands and set them beside the brownies. "Where is everyone?"

"Melody's still napping," Nick answered. "Zach and Patrick are out in the backyard scoping out where they want to build a tree house."

"Maybe I should take Annie and Belle out to see how they're doing," Jeff suggested.

"That's a good idea," Cece agreed. "That way I can help Nick in here."

Jeff sandwiched himself between the two little girls and led them to the back door. While Cece transferred food from the cooler to the refrigerator, Nick attempted to clear the clutter from the kitchen table.

"It's a bit of a mess in here. I'm not sure about dinner..." he said apologetically.

"Don't worry." She dismissed his concern with a wave of her hand. "We'll eat outside. Everything's already made except for the hot dogs, and Jeff can put them on the grill." She lifted a corner of the curtain covering the window. "Oh, good. You have a picnic table."

"I guess completely furnished means completely furnished," Nick commented, moving one of the cardboard boxes onto the floor so that Cece could have space to work on the counter. "I'm not sure what's inside the cupboards or what I need to unpack from these boxes."

"Here. Let me check it out and see what you have," She opened cupboards and drawers at random. Before she had finished her inventory, Annabelle appeared.

"You're never going to guess what I heard," the older woman said anxiously.

"Mom always gets the latest town gossip because she works at the post office," Cece told Nick.

"I didn't hear this at work," Annabelle interjected. "I ran into Gina Santori at Marge's Diner, and she's the one who told me."

"Told you what, Mother?" Cece faced her with her hands on her hips.

"That some big Hollywood agent is in town looking for a baby to star in a TV commercial."

Nick, who had been shoving pots and pans into a cupboard, nearly bumped his head as he jerked upright. "What Hollywood agent?" he asked.

"Her name is Kika Mancini, and she's staying at the lodge," Annabelle announced with authority.

A picture of one shapely blonde with a beguiling look in her eyes formed in Nick's mind.

"Apparently she was here last week and stayed at Granny Rose's Bed-and-Breakfast. That's how Gina heard about it."

"Why would she come to Tyler to look for a baby?" Cece wondered aloud. Nick knew the answer, but didn't volunteer any information. Personally, he didn't want to think about Kika Mancini.

"According to Gina, she saw one of Glenna's videos and was impressed with the babies in them," Annabelle explained. "Dolores says she has to type up a notice for the paper tomorrow giving all the details." Dolores Larson was a good friend of Annabelle's, who worked at the *Tyler Citizen*.

Nick shifted uneasily. "She's wasting her time."

"Why is Dolores wasting her time?" Annabelle asked in a puzzled voice.

"I'm not talking about Dolores, Annabelle." Nick controlled his impatience. "I'm talking about the casting agent."

"What makes you say that?" Cece inquired.

Nick shrugged. "Look at the size of Tyler. I can't imagine that she'd find a star here."

"Better not say that around the mothers of Tyler!" Annabelle exclaimed. "We may not be Los Angeles, California, but there are some mighty fine-looking babies in this little town."

Nick could see that he had offended his mother-in-law and quickly attempted to make amends. "Of course there are. It has nothing to do with the children of Tyler. It's the parents. I don't think people around these parts are gullible enough to fall for some casting agent telling them she can make their children stars."

"How old a child is she looking for?" Cece asked.

"They're going to audition girls between eighteen and twenty-four months," Annabelle answered.

"That excludes the twins," Cece said with a bit of disappointment. "Melody could try out, though," she suggested to Nick. "She's darling."

"Maybe, but modeling is not something I want to encourage."

"Doing one baby commercial is not exactly modeling," Cece responded.

"The thought of a baby working..." He shook his head in disapproval.

"I'm not sure it's actually work," Cece continued. "There are child-labor laws to protect the rights of children. They can only be on camera a short time each day. That's why they use twins so often when they're filming TV shows."

"Still, I don't think it's a good idea." Nick grimaced. "Children are forced to grow up much too fast nowadays. Exposing them to the glitter of a world populated with phony people only speeds up the process. I wouldn't want any of my kids subjected to such a life-style."

"I'm glad to hear you say that." Annabelle patted him on the back. "Melody has too gentle a spirit to be in with those Hollywood types."

"Hollywood types? Mother, they're looking for a baby for a commercial, not the movies," Cece said patiently.

"I know, but Evelyn Palmer told me that when her niece's daughter got involved in child modeling, she had nothing but trouble. The girl started having problems at school and none of her friends would play with her after that. She got tagged as being stuck-up."

"I don't think that would be a problem for Melody. She's only a baby," Cece argued.

"It's no kind of life for a child of any age. All that makeup and those lights . . ." Annabelle frowned. "I think Nick's right. The folks of Tyler know better than to get their kids into such an unsavory business."

"None of the parents at TylerTots objected to Glenna making the videos," Cece said reasonably.

"But that's different. Glenna treats them with loving care and there isn't anything artificial about what she's doing," Annabelle insisted.

"I'm not so sure I see the difference," Cece admitted.

"Of course there's a difference," her mother exclaimed.

"It really doesn't matter, does it?" Nick asked a bit impatiently. "Whatever this Mancini woman is doing in Tyler, it's not going to affect any of us."

"But it will affect someone—that's the point. Anyone who has a little girl is thinking this might be the answer to a prayer," Annabelle contended. "People who normally wouldn't be interested in putting their kids in show business might do so out of desperation."

"You mean because of the fire at the F and M?" Nick inquired.

"There are quite a few families who have been out of work."

"It'll probably be a nine days' wonder and blow over," Cece predicted.

"I hope you're right," her mother replied, then stuck her head out the window and ordered Jeff to start the grill so they could get the hot dogs cooking.

But long after the subject was dismissed, Nick found himself thinking about the blond casting director. It had been a long time since any woman had caused such a strong and immediate physical reaction in him. It made him wonder if maybe he should start dating again.

Of course, he knew that if and when he ever became interested in another woman, it would be someone quiet and gentle like Beth, not a fast talker like Kika Mancini.

KIKA WAS NOT ONE to accept no for an answer. Just because Nick Miller had told her he wasn't interested in having Melody audition to become Fancy's Baby didn't mean it wasn't going to happen. All Kika needed to do was convince him of the wonderful opportunity this was for his daughter.

Of course, it wasn't going to be easy. Kika would have to be persuasive, yet cautiously so. Although he appeared to be rather reserved, she knew that beneath that cool exterior lurked a man who carried handcuffs and a blindfold in his suitcase when he traveled.

Thanks to Susannah Santori, she had learned that Nick had rented the old Watson place on Elm Street near the edge of town. As soon as she had finished posting announcements of the audition in all the local establishments around town, she paid him a visit.

When she arrived at the picturesque two-story home, there was no answer to her knock on the front door. She followed the walk around to the back.

Sitting in a sandbox was Melody and a boy Kika assumed was her older brother, for he had the same shade of red hair as the toddler. Kika leaned over the white picket fence and said, "I'm looking for Nick Miller. Is he home?"

The boy jumped up, and a shower of sand fell from his jean shorts. "He's in the house getting gum out of Patrick's hair."

"Would you tell him I'd like to see him when he's done?" Kika requested, wondering if Patrick was yet another of Nick Miller's children.

The boy ran over to the basement window, knelt down and shouted, "Dad, there's a lady here to see you." Kika watched him nod, then run back over to the fence and open the gate for her.

"He says he'll be out in a few minutes." He waved her inside. "Come on in."

There were several lawn chairs in the shade of an old oak tree, but Kika opted for a wooden corner seat on the sandbox.

"Hi, Melody. How are you?"

Melody didn't say a word, but neither did she look away.

"You know my sister?" the boy asked, eyeing Kika curiously.

"Yes, we met at TylerTots," she answered, reaching for a plastic shovel. "What are we making?"

"I think it's a town," the boy answered. "Melody hasn't told me for sure, but she's moving those little cars along what looks to be a road."

"Aha," Kika said in understanding.

"Are you a friend of my dad's?" the boy asked.

"Oh, I'm sorry. I should have introduced myself. I'm Kika Mancini." She offered her hand to the child, who took it without hesitation.

"I'm Zachary Miller. I'm nine." He pumped her hand briefly, then dropped it. "I've never heard the name Kika before."

"It's Italian."

"Oh. We're Heinz."

"Heinz?"

He nodded. "You know—fifty-seven flavors. We're all sorts of stuff—English, Irish, Norwegian. Grandma says we're mostly German."

"I see."

"Are you from the day-care center?"

"No, I'm just visiting Tyler. Actually, I'm here on business. I'm looking for a little girl to star in a TV commercial."

"Are you the Hollywood lady who's going to make some kid in Tyler rich?" His eyes widened.

"I'm not from Hollywood, but I have worked with some of the people there."

"You know movie stars?"

"A few."

"Do you know Jim Carrey?"

"I've met him, yes."

"Really?" His eyes grew even wider.

"Yes, really. He's a funny man, isn't he?"

"He's cool!" After a few moments Zachary said, "Everyone's been talking about the posters you've put up around town. Are you really going to choose someone from Tyler to be on TV?"

"That's why I'm here. Of course, it all depends on what happens at the audition," Kika answered. "Hopefully, one lucky Tyler tot will be the next Fancy's Baby." As she said the words, she looked at Melody, who continued to stare back at her without so much as a smile or a frown…just an innocent gaze.

"What kind of a baby are you looking for?" Zachary wanted to know.

"One we can use in a baby-furniture commercial. Someone who can sit in a children's rocker, lie on a youth bed—that sort of thing."

"Will the baby have to talk?"

"Umm-hmm, but just a couple of words."

A look of disappointment crossed his face. "It figures. I was hoping Melody could try out."

"She can."

"But she doesn't talk."

"She doesn't have to say much. Just the word *fancy.*" Kika looked at the little girl and said, "You can say *fancy,* can't you, Melody?"

Again there was no response.

"She can't say anything," Zach told her.

Kika looked at the beautiful little girl. She herself was no authority on childhood development, but all the babies she had auditioned thus far had vocabularies ranging anywhere from half a dozen to hundreds of words.

"She doesn't talk," Kika repeated, suddenly understanding why Nick Miller hadn't wanted to pursue the audition. Why hadn't he just told her he had reservations because his daughter hadn't developed her vocabulary?

"Dad's had her to the doctor and they said nothing's wrong with her voice. She's just doesn't want to talk," Zach informed Kika in a very adultlike manner. "Grandma thinks it's because of our upbringing, but Dad says Grandma doesn't always know the answer to everything."

The sound of a screen door slamming had Kika's head turning in the direction of the house. Nick Miller was striding toward her, an angry look on his face.

"Ms. Mancini," he said gruffly.

Kika stood up, refusing to be intimidated by his glare. "I was just having a chat with your children, Mr. Miller. Zachary is a very interesting child."

Zachary beamed at the praise and moved closer to Kika, smiling up at her avidly.

"Zach, would you go inside and see if your brother's all right?" It was more of an order than a request.

"Do I have to?" he asked with a frown.

"Zach, go." It was a command this time.

"Goodbye, Kika," Zach said, clearly smitten with their guest.

As soon as he was out of sight, Nick said, "I don't think we have anything further to discuss, Ms. Mancini."

"I thought we had agreed it was Kika," she said warmly, ignoring the frostiness of his tone. "And I hoped you'd give me a few more minutes of your time."

"I'm not interested in Melody trying out for any commercial," he stated in no uncertain terms.

"You won't have to travel all the way to Minneapolis. There's going to be a crew coming out next week, to do the taping right here in Tyler."

"I told you I'm not interested."

"Please don't say that, Mr. Miller. She's a beautiful child and this could be a wonderful opportunity for her."

"No."

"If you're concerned because Melody isn't talking yet, you don't need to be."

His eyes darkened and his brow furrowed. "Maybe you don't understand the word *no*, Ms. Mancini."

Melody had been watching the two adults from her spot in the sandbox. As her father's voice grew louder, her eyes widened. When his last "no" came out with resounding finality, she burst into tears.

Nick lifted her into his arms to comfort her. "I think you'd better be going, Ms. Mancini."

"I'm sorry," Kika apologized. "I didn't mean to upset her." She wished there was something she could do to comfort the little girl, but at this point it was obvious the only thing to do was leave.

As she started for the gate, she saw Zach in the kitchen window. She went out of her way to walk past him.

"Bye, Zach. It was nice meeting you," she said through the screen.

"Too bad you can't stay." He held a pair of handcuffs. "Dad's going to show us how to do magic tricks with these."

Magic tricks. Was that why Nick Miller had handcuffs and a blindfold in his suitcase? Even though she hadn't accomplished her goal to get Melody to audition, Kika had a smile on her face as she drove away.

CHAPTER FOUR

IT DIDN'T TAKE Nick long to realize that in a town the size of Tyler, news spread faster than germs. At the front of the news brigade was his mother-in-law, a fact he discovered the following morning when she corralled him on a street corner and steered him into Marge's Diner for a cup of coffee.

"Annabelle, this isn't a good time for me. The kids..." He tried to excuse himself, but she wasn't about to be deterred.

"The kids are fine. Abby's perfectly capable of watching them for another thirty minutes," she told him, aware of the fact that he had hired the teenage girl next door to baby-sit while he ran errands in town. Annabelle shoved him onto one of the stools at the counter while several pairs of eyes watched.

"Why didn't you tell me that Mancini woman is here because of Melody?" she demanded in a loud enough voice that Nick was pretty certain even the kitchen help could hear.

"She's not."

"I talked to Glenna McRoberts today."

"Then you know Kika Mancini is here because of the videos Glenna produces," Nick said calmly.

"And the fact that she had seen Melody on that video, right?" His mother-in-law pinned him with her intimidating stare. "She came all the way to Tyler hoping to get Melody for that commercial, didn't she?''

"You'd have to ask her that question," he said, hoping his near whisper would cause her to lower her voice. Almost every head in the place was cocked in his direction. In the short time he had been in Tyler he had learned that when Annabelle talked, people listened.

"Glenna says you met with this Mancini woman at TylerTots." Again, her voice held an accusation.

He sighed. "I saw her when I dropped off Melody. It was not an arranged meeting."

"So it's true then?"

"What's true?" he asked a bit impatiently.

"That she's bringing the film crew here because of you?"

Just then Marge interrupted them, a coffee carafe in hand. "You two gonna have breakfast or just coffee?"

"Bring me one of those caramel rolls, will you?" Annabelle answered.

"Welcome to Tyler, Nick," Marge said as she poured him the cup of black coffee he requested. "I would imagine it's quite different from what you're used to in California."

"Yes, but it's a nice kind of different," he said sincerely.

"I suppose all this Hollywood stuff is nothing new to you," Marge remarked, leaning a hip against the counter. "I can't believe the commotion this Fancy's Baby thing is causing, can you?" Her question was addressed to Annabelle.

"It's no wonder. There are posters everywhere."

"She's got plenty of people talking, that's for sure," Marge commented.

"Everyone thinks it's their kid who's going to get a big break," Annabelle said with disdain.

"The word is that some lucky family in Tyler could end up millionaires." There was awe in Marge's voice.

Nick shifted uneasily. "It's only a commercial, not a lottery winning."

"Just last week there was something on one of the talk shows about getting into commercials and making lots of money," Marge added, obviously undaunted.

"That's right. All it takes is one clever advertisement and—" Annabelle snapped her fingers "—instant fame."

"I don't think that's going to happen with the Fancy baby," Nick said soberly.

"Maybe, maybe not," Marge said pensively. "Of course, to the folks around here it doesn't matter. With so many people being out of work, the thought of a baby making extra money is a tempting one."

"Well, there definitely won't be a shortage of babies at that audition," Annabelle agreed. "There are too many hungry mouths."

"What about your little granddaughter? Is she going to try out?"

Nick gave Annabelle a look that dared her to contradict him. She didn't. "Melody's not the type for commercials," she said in an almost gentle voice.

Any animosity Nick had been harboring for his mother-in-law dissolved. It warmed his heart to know that Annabelle's voice softened whenever she spoke about Melody. It made him think that he had done the right thing coming to Tyler. Melody needed a woman's love.

"I hear this little Italian gal is quite a looker," Marge said, her eyes on Nick as if gauging his reaction.

"She's too perky if you ask me. I've always been suspicious of perky people," Annabelle answered.

"When did you meet her?" Nick asked his mother-in-law.

"She stopped in the post office this morning. Wanted to know if we had overnight mail service." Annabelle harrumphed again. "Where does she think she is? In Mayberry?"

Both women laughed. Nick didn't want to admit that he had wondered the same thing. Was Tyler a large enough community to provide express mail service?

"By the way, what's the latest word on Tisha?"

"She's getting stronger every day," Annabelle told the owner of the diner. For Nick's benefit she added, "Tisha Olsen owns the beauty shop down the street. She had a heart attack last month, but she's going to be all right."

"I hope she's up and about in time for the weddings."

"I figure she'll make Sheila Lawson's in August for sure."

"She wanted to do something special for Glenna's, but that's only a few weeks away. Well, I'd better get back to work," Marge said when the short-order cook called out to her. "It's good seeing you, Nick." With a little wave, she was gone.

Nick expected that having Annabelle for a mother-in-law was going to speed up the process of getting to know people in Tyler. Before they finished their coffee, she had introduced him to everyone in the restaurant. Which was just as well, Nick figured, since they had all heard the conversation about Kika Mancini.

On the way out of the café Annabelle suggested he might be interested in meeting some of the single parents of Tyler. Nick had a hunch she meant the mothers, not the fathers.

What he didn't need was a matchmaking mother-in-law. If and when he ever started dating again, he wanted to choose with whom. Unbidden came the memory of Kika Mancini sitting on a miniature chair with her blond hair swishing across her bare shoulders.

She looked like a million bucks, but she was not a woman any single father should be interested in. She made a living selling kids to the entertainment industry, and he had three children.

So why was he still thinking about her?

BECAUSE IT WAS the start of the Fourth of July holiday, Granny Rose's Bed-and-Breakfast was booked solid by the time Kika decided to return to Tyler. Thanks to Susannah Santori's efforts, however, she was able to get a room at Timberlake Lodge.

Located about twenty minutes' drive from Tyler, the former private hunting lodge had earned its reputation as a wonderful getaway for those looking for the quiet charm of the country. Susannah's husband, Joe, had completed the renovations, managing to retain the lodge's rustic appeal yet still modernizing it so that it would be attractive to guests. Several new wings had been added when the Addison Hotel chain had purchased the lodge from its longtime owner, Tyler industrialist Judson Ingalls, yet it didn't have the feel of a big hotel.

The minute Kika walked in the front door and saw the chandelier made of deer antlers, she knew she was going to like the place. It had character and atmosphere, as well as every convenience known to travelers.

At first Kika had been hesitant about staying anywhere but in Tyler, but after talking to Sheila Lawson, the lodge's manager, she decided it would feel more like a holiday if she stayed here rather than in a motel. On the first morning of her stay, however, she began to question whether she had made the right decision.

Strange sounds came from the forest surrounding the lodge. Taking a walk down to the lake, Kika was surprised to again hear the sound that had woken her. It was yodeling. She knew the lodge was bordered by farms, but not once in her twenty-eight years had she heard any of the Minnesota farmers yodeling in the morning. If someone had warned her she might hear a mooing cow at the lodge, she wouldn't have been surprised. But yodeling?

It had been three days since the ad soliciting tryouts for the Fancy's Baby model had appeared in the *Tyler Citizen* and the posters had been hung. Eager to see the sign-up sheet, Kika drove to TylerTots immediately after breakfast.

"Glenna. It's good to see you." She greeted the day-care worker with a smile. "I've come to see how many names we have so far."

Glenna ushered her into the office and handed her a clipboard. "It looks like around forty."

Kika's eyes scanned the list of names. As she expected, Melody Miller was not among them. "It looks as if so far everyone is from Tyler."

"A lot of those names are kids from the center. I'm sure once people in the surrounding communities get wind of the audition, they'll start calling in, too," Glenna told her.

"I really appreciate your help with this. I figure since nearly everyone knows you because of your video business, you'd be the perfect one for them to contact. I hope it hasn't interfered with your work here?"

"Oh, no, not at all. Angela's been good about letting me do the videos. Fortunately, there's enough of us here that we can manage."

Kika glanced out at the play area and saw that Angela Murphy and one of her assistants were glancing curiously toward the office. The only staff member who didn't seem interested was Daphne Sullivan.

The first time Kika visited TylerTots she had learned that Daphne had a two-year-old named Jennifer, who hadn't been in any of the Playmates videos. Kika looked once more at the list and remarked, "I don't see Jennifer Sullivan's name on here."

"I think Daphne's a little shy about stuff like this. When she started working here she asked if we would mind not including Jennifer in the videos," Glenna told her.

"First it's Melody's father, now it's Jennifer's mother." Kika shook her head in amazement. "Normally I have to discourage people, not encourage them."

"I can talk to Daphne if you'd like," Glenna offered.

Kika shook her head. "No, it's all right. It looks as if we're going to have a full schedule the way it is."

"When will the film crew arrive?" Glenna asked curiously.

"A week from tomorrow. I need to arrange for a place for them to stay. Sheila Lawson told me once the Fourth of July has passed she'll have room at the lodge."

"Independence Day is a big celebration here. Every year we have a parade and a picnic in the park," Glenna explained. "This year there's a carnival coming to town, plus fireworks to end the day."

"It sounds like fun. I love a parade."

"I'm surprised they haven't asked you to be in it."

Kika laughed. "Certainly I'm not a celebrity."

"No, but your presence has generated a lot of excitement. I'm going to have a float with some of the Tyler tots who've been in my Video Playmates series."

"You are? Cool!"

"You're welcome to ride along."

Again Kika laughed. "I think I'd better watch from the sidelines."

Glenna shrugged. "Suit yourself, but it might be a good chance to check out the babies sitting on the curb watching the parade go by."

Kika didn't want to tell her that the only baby she needed to check out she could find without riding down Main Street on a float. She had but one mission for the Fourth of July celebration and that was to get Nick Miller to agree to bring Melody to the audition. If that didn't happen, fireworks or no fireworks, Kika's Fourth of July would be a big dud.

BECAUSE OF the holiday celebrations, breakfast hours in the lodge's dining room were shortened on the morning of the Fourth. Unable to resist a swim in the clear water of the lake, Kika skipped her usual blueberry pancakes, thinking she'd pick up something in town.

Dressed in a pair of white shorts and a red sleeveless shirt, she pulled her hair back and tied it with a blue-and-white-striped bandanna, then grabbed her camera and headed out the door. By the time she arrived in town, however, most of the eating establishments were closed so that their employees could watch the parade.

The citizens of Tyler lined the streets. Some sat on lawn chairs, others on blankets, still others on the bare curb. Kika walked up and down Main Street, trying to find Nick Miller and his children. She was about to give up when she noticed Melody atop her father's shoulders. They were at the very end of the parade route, near the town Square.

Across the street from Nick and his family were the Santoris. Kika pushed her way through the crowd until she was next to the innkeepers.

"Mind if I join you?"

"Kika! How good to see you! Is it working out for you at the lodge?"

"Umm-hmm, it's great, although I miss that wonderful feather bed of yours."

She and Susannah exchanged pleasantries until the sound of a marching band heralded the start of the parade. Cub Scout troops, war veterans and elected civic officials filed past, waving to the crowd.

"Oh, look. That must be the convention of yodelers," Susannah exclaimed as a group of men in le-

derhosen marched down the street. "Sheila Lawson
said they were staying at the lodge."

"You don't have to tell me. I wake up to that every
morning," Kika told her as the group yodeled their
way past them.

Several times during the parade, Kika looked at
Nick, but even though she was certain he saw her, he
didn't acknowledge her presence. Sitting in the sun,
she began to feel rather light-headed. She closed her
eyes briefly to try to keep her senses on an even keel.

Fire trucks rolled by with their sirens blaring,
snapping Kika to attention. Celebrities perched on
convertibles waved as they passed, but it was a flatbed
trailer pulled by a tractor that drew the most ap-
plause from the crowd. From it Judson Ingalls traveled the parade route, hopping off occasionally to
spread the good news to various employees that the
rebuilding of Ingalls Farm and Machinery would start
next week. Kika learned from Susannah that now that
the insurance company had determined last winter's
fire was not arson, the plant would be rebuilt and
employees could finally have hope of returning to
work.

Shortly after the F and M entry, the TylerTots float
came by. All the toddlers on the fake grass wore red
T-shirts that said I'm a Tyler Tot and they carried
miniature flags.

Kika unzipped her camera case. Because the sun
was in front of her, she crossed the street to eliminate
its glare. As she stooped to capture all of the tiny tots
in the picture, she felt dizzy again. Whether it was
from the heat or from a lack of food, she wasn't sure.
The last thing she remembered was Glenna waving at
her.

When she awoke she was lying in the grass in the shade. A woman with short dark hair and gray eyes held her wrist.

"My name is Cece Baron. I'm a nurse," the woman said, as she took her pulse. "How are you feeling?"

"I'm fine. What happened?" she asked. She attempted to sit, but Cece insisted she lie still.

"You fainted during the parade."

Behind Cece stood Susannah, anxiously awaiting the diagnosis. "Is she going to be all right?" Kika heard her ask Cece as she handed the nurse a cold cloth.

"Her vital signs are normal," Cece answered, placing the cloth across Kika's forehead.

"I'm fine," Kika insisted. "I don't know why I would have passed out like that. It's never happened to me before."

"Then you don't have anything in your medical history that would have caused you to faint?" Cece asked.

"Oh, no."

"Maybe she ate something that didn't agree with her," Susannah suggested.

"I haven't eaten anything since yesterday afternoon," Kika confessed. Then, seeing the admonishing look on Cece's face, she added, "I've been too busy."

"That's probably the problem. No food in your stomach, the hot sun..." Cece looked up at Susannah.

"I'll go get her something," the innkeeper offered.

"No, it's all right. Susannah, you go back to Joe and Gina. You're missing the parade," Kika told her.

"Are you sure you don't want me to get you something to eat first?" Susannah asked.

"No, I feel fine. See?" This time Kika did sit up. "I can get myself something to eat." She attempted to stand, but her wobbly legs had her gingerly easing herself back down.

"I'm on the picnic committee. Since I was about to go over and help with the food, why don't you come along and we'll see what we can find?" Cece suggested in a serene voice.

Something in her soft-spoken manner made Kika want to trust her. "That's very kind of you, but I've already been enough trouble."

"I have ulterior motives," Cece confessed. "The picnic committee can use another pair of hands to get the food out on the tables. You'll earn your meal."

"All right." They sat for several minutes longer while Kika sipped a soda and slowly regained her strength. When she no longer felt unsure of her legs, she stood, dusting off her white shorts.

"How did I get here? The last thing I remember was standing in the middle of the street taking a picture of the TylerTots float."

"Oh, that's right. I wonder what happened to your camera?" Cece remarked with a worried frown, looking about the grassy area. "Hopefully, it'll turn up."

"How did I get here?"

"My brother-in-law saw you fall. He sent my nephew to get me and carried you over here to the shade."

"That was very kind of him. You'll have to point him out to me at the picnic so I can thank him."

"He would have stayed and made sure you were okay, but he needed to get back to my mom, who had five grandchildren in her care. Besides, I knew you would feel more comfortable without a strange man fussing over you."

Again, Kika felt herself drawn to this gentle woman. "Thank you. You're right. It's rather embarrassing."

"Don't feel bad. You're not the only one who's succumbed to the heat. My husband, Jeff, is a doctor, and he's been treating members of the marching band all morning. I think we're going to set a record."

As they crossed the grassy park, Cece talked about the schedule of events for the rest of the day. Kika couldn't help but admire the way everyone in the small town pulled together to make the holiday celebration a community event.

"The only thing different this year," Cece told her, "is that the carnival's come to town. I imagine that instead of watching the softball games, many of the kids will be over there."

Their destination was a small group of women gathered around a row of picnic tables. "I've recruited another volunteer," Cece announced as they approached the group. "Only she needs to eat first, then work."

Kika could see the curiosity in the eyes of the women, but each gave her a warm smile and welcomed her to the picnic committee.

"I want you to know, Kika, that you are looking at the women responsible for putting on the best picnic in the whole state of Wisconsin." Cece proceeded to introduce them one by one.

"Amanda Trask, my sister-in-law, a wonderful attorney and the reason we have hot dogs for this occasion." The chestnut-haired, blue-eyed woman offered Kika her hand.

"Alyssa Wocheck, my mother-in-law, president of the Women's Garden Club and involved in nearly every civic event in Tyler." Kika shook her hand as Cece added, "She's managed to procure two-hundred pounds of hamburger patties.

"And this is Marge Phelps, owner of Marge's Diner. She's this year's committee chairwoman. We figured who better for the job than someone who feeds people every day of the year?"

Kika recognized the woman from having eaten at the diner.

Cece moved on, saying "Anna Kelsey, of Kelsey Boardinghouse. She recently became a grandma—yet again. Her daughter-in-law Pam had a baby girl last week. If we run out of potato salad, we blame her.

"And last but not least, Britt Marshack, owner of Yes! Yogurt. She organized the ice-cream social. In addition to pie and ice cream, we'll be having Britt's scrumptious cheesecake and, of course, Yes! Yogurt."

"Pleased to meet you. All of you," Kika said sincerely.

While the women went about setting out the food, Kika sampled the potato salad and had a piece of watermelon. Being the good nurse and mother she was, Cece made sure Kika was adequately fed before allowing her to lend a hand.

By the time the parade had ended and the towns-folk had meandered over to the park, hot dogs and hamburgers were on the grills, the picnic tables were covered with all sorts of wonderful potluck dishes and the park lawn had become a patchwork quilt of blankets and families ready to eat.

"What can I do to help?" Kika finally asked, tossing her watermelon rind in a trashcan.

"You're a guest, Kika. I was only teasing when I said you needed to work for your food," Cece answered.

"But I want to help."

"I'll put you in charge of the beverage cart, but only on one condition—that you agree to picnic with my family." Cece pointed to a tall man with two little girls. "That's them over there."

"How cool! Twins! How old are they?" Kika asked.

"Three. Too old to be Fancy's Baby, right?"

"Sorry." Kika smiled apologetically.

"I'm glad you're going to be joining us. I'm curious to hear all about your work," Cece said sincerely.

Kika felt as though an instant bond had been formed between the two of them. She hadn't expected to develop such a kinship with the quiet-spoken nurse, nor had she expected the women of Tyler to accept her as one of their own. She found herself giggling and chatting as people came to fill their plates at the picnic feast. As she glanced across the park and saw a sea of happy people sitting on blankets, she felt as if she were in a Norman Rockwell painting.

"It's time to grab a plate and sit down," Cece told her after they had been serving food for nearly an hour.

"Has everyone been fed?" Kika knew that Nick Miller and his family hadn't come through the serving line. She had watched for them.

"No, but our replacements are here."

Kika couldn't believe her eyes. Standing behind the picnic committee were five men with aprons wrapped around their middles.

"Tyler's an equal-opportunity community," Cece said with a grin.

"I'm impressed." Kika gave her own apron to a young man named Jeremy, then for the second time that day helped herself to the food.

Jeff Baron, she soon discovered, was just as nice as his wife, making her feel right at home on the patchwork quilt. Kika learned that he was chief of staff at Tyler General and that Cece no longer worked as a nurse but stayed home with their daughters.

Kika was in the middle of explaining her work to Jeff when Cece looked over her shoulder and said, "Kika, you're going to get that opportunity to thank my brother-in-law. He's coming now."

Kika turned around and saw Nick Miller approaching. One hand held Melody's, the other balanced a plate of food. The two boys carried their own lunches. Walking beside them was the woman Kika recognized as the postmistress. She carried two plates.

"Hey, Dad! Look! It's Kika!" Zachary proclaimed when he caught sight of the casting director.

Nick's eyes followed his son's pointing finger. There on a blanket with his sister-in-law sat Kika

Mancini. The sight of her was like a shot of adrenaline.

"The boys have met her, too?" Annabelle's voice held accusation.

"She's really cool, Grandma. She knows Jim Carrey," Zachary boasted.

Jim Carrey. They did travel in different worlds, Nick realized.

"Nick, come meet Kika." Cece jumped up to spread another quilt on the ground.

"He's already met Ms. Mancini," Annabelle snapped, before barking out orders as to where her grandchildren should sit.

Seeing the surprise on Cece's face, Kika said, "We met at the day-care center." To Nick she said, "I understand I owe you a thank-you."

"Dad picked you up when you fainted," Zachary announced proudly.

"Are you all right?" Nick wished his own head didn't feel so light simply because he could see the delicious curve of thigh exposed by Kika's shorts.

"I'm fine. Cece is a good nurse." Before they could say another word to each other, Cece introduced her mother.

"Maybe you should be lying down if you're not feeling well," Annabelle suggested, running her eyes over Kika's slender figure.

"Mother, Kika's fine," Cece insisted. "And I'm sure she doesn't want to miss the fun."

Fun? Nick wondered how the afternoon could be anything but agony if Kika Mancini was going to look like a pinup girl from World War II. Until he had seen her in shorts he hadn't realized what a great pair of legs she had. Now it was all he seemed to notice.

"Kika, do you play softball?" Cece inquired.

"Not on a regular basis, but I have three brothers so I've had plenty of experience," she answered.

"One of the regulars on the downtown merchants' team has to sit on the bench because of a back injury. My guess is they'd be delighted to find a replacement," Cece said enthusiastically.

Nick thought that if the team was composed mainly of men, the players would be falling over their feet trying to make Kika welcome.

"Are we going to be able to run in the races, Dad?" Zachary asked, interrupting Nick's musings.

"We'll see," he answered, which drew Annabelle into their conversation.

"Of course you can run," she told her grandson. "There are all sorts of prizes to be given away." She looked at Nick and said, "If you won't take the boys, I will."

"I'll do it," he told her, thinking it probably best that he watch the children's footraces rather than the adult softball tourney. Still, he couldn't prevent the twinge of envy he experienced when the softball captains began to gather their players. As Kika sauntered off with a mitt dangling from her wrist, he wished he didn't have to watch six-year-olds running for the finish line. He wanted to be the catcher squatting behind home plate when Kika stepped up to bat.

CHAPTER FIVE

KIKA SHOULD HAVE known Nick Miller wouldn't be at the softball games. He was new to Tyler. Plus he didn't look like the type who liked to play ball. Actually, he looked as if he didn't know how to have much fun at all.

Which made Kika wonder if the Miller children were enjoying the picnic. Something about them tugged at her emotions. Maybe it was the fact that instead of a mother's love they had a grandmother who looked as though she could breathe fire.

As the sun made its gradual descent toward the horizon, families began drifting over to the carnival site. Kika hoped the Millers would be one of those families.

After nearly circling the carnival area without seeing them, she was beginning to think that Nick had taken his children home. Then she spotted the two boys gawking at an amusement ride called The Rocket. Not far behind them was their father, standing in line at the ticket kiosk sandwiched between the carousel and the Ferris wheel.

Kika hadn't ridden a carousel since she'd been a child. Assuming Nick was buying a ticket for Melody to ride one of the brightly painted horses, she got in line behind him.

"Hello again," she said with a friendly grin.

He acknowledged her greeting with a nod. Melody, who was in his arms, turned her head toward his shoulder. Except for a shy peek at Kika, she kept her face hidden.

Kika refused to be discouraged. "Are you having a good time?"

Nick shrugged. "Not bad. It's a little noisy."

"Zachary and Patrick look like they're enjoying themselves," she commented, glancing over to where Nick's sons stared with mouths agape at the tumbling rocket.

"I think you have to be under thirty to like spinning around upside down," he remarked as the two boys watched the rocket catapult up and over.

"Aw, come on, Mr. Miller. If you talk like that I'm going to think you don't know how to have any fun," Kika said, a challenge in her voice.

She expected that statement would end their conversation. It didn't.

"How were the softball games?" he asked.

"We lost, but I had fun."

"Is that your consolation prize?" he asked, looking at the white teddy bear she carried under her arm. Melody, too, was casting furtive looks at the stuffed animal.

She held up the plush bear. "I won this by tossing a dime onto a dinner plate at one of the game booths, but only after I spent probably twice as much as it's worth. And the worse part is I have to lug this bear around with me the rest of the night."

Their conversation ended as Nick stepped up to the kiosk. As soon as he had purchased his tickets and moved away, Kika said to the saleswoman, "I want one of whatever it was he bought."

To Kika's dismay, she discovered her ride ticket was not for the carousel to the left of the kiosk, but the Ferris wheel to the right. Kika stared at the gigantic spinning wheel and felt a moment of panic.

Spinning motion she could handle, but heights were enough to cause her heart to palpitate and her palms to sweat. She debated whether the Fancy account was worth putting herself in a tiny gondola suspended from a giant wheel.

"Have your tickets ready," the attendant announced as one by one the seats on the Ferris wheel emptied and a new set of passengers boarded. Kika saw the Miller family move toward the entrance. Taking a deep breath, she followed them.

Zachary and Patrick were the first ones on, shouting and waving to their father as they slowly moved up the giant wheel.

When it came time for Nick and Melody to board, the attendant looked at Kika and asked, "Are you alone?" When she nodded, he said, "Then you're gonna have to ride with them." He gestured for her to get in beside Nick and Melody.

Perfect, Kika thought. She couldn't have planned it any better. Now all she needed to do was control her fear of heights and everything would be fine.

As she climbed in beside Nick, she forced herself to smile. When the safety bar was locked in place, Kika's nerves twanged. With a jerk, the car began its ascent, gently swaying back and forth.

Kika knew the only way she could keep from panicking would be to avoid looking down. Instead of viewing the panorama spread out below them, she focused on little Melody, who was sitting in between the two adults looking very grown-up. Since they were the second-to-last passengers to get on, there was only one more jerky stop before the Ferris wheel began its rotational journey. If it wasn't for the fact that they were high above the ground, Kika would have enjoyed the sensation created by the up-and-down motion. The July air was warm and humid, and the movement created a welcome breeze against her skin.

"Wheeeee . . ." Kika looked at the toddler, giving her a smile. "Isn't this fun?"

In answer Melody turned her face into her father's polo shirt. That prompted Nick to say, "Look, Melody. You can see Grandma's house from here." He stretched out his arm, but Kika's eyes refused to follow.

The Ferris wheel had made only three orbits when there was a sudden jerk, followed by a screeching sound. Although the neon lights burned brightly, the cars came to a halt.

"What's happening?" Kika asked Nick, her voice faltering with fear.

"It looks like we've stopped."

"Well, I can see that. The question is why. No one's getting on or off, are they?" Kika had to ask Nick that question, for there was no way she would look to the ground to see for herself.

"No."

There was a collective buzz of commotion from the other Ferris wheel passengers. Kika could hear Zachary calling out to his father. "Yo, Dad. We're over here."

Kika saw Nick turn around in his seat to look across the giant wheel. "You and Patrick sit still, okay? Everything's going to be all right."

Kika heard a loud clang, then a sound like an engine grinding. The neon lights trimming the spokes of the ferris wheel went out.

"Everybody just stay where you are," the attendant shouted up to them. "We've lost power but it's only temporary. I'm sure everything will be working just fine in a few minutes."

"Are we stuck up here?" Kika asked, trying not to panic at the thought.

"It probably won't be for long," Nick answered, settling back in the seat.

Kika closed her eyes, willing her mind to go blank. She visualized that she wasn't halfway up a Ferris wheel, but sitting in her car with the windows wide open.

After several minutes had passed and there was still no life in the amusement ride, Zachary called out to his father, "Hey, Dad. Are we going to have to be rescued by firemen with ladders?"

So much for creative visualization, Kika thought. It was bad enough being suspended in the air, but the mere thought of having to climb down a ladder propped against the metal frame had her tightening her grip on the safety bar.

"I doubt that it will come to that."

Nick's words did little to reassure Kika. "Can't you do something?" she pleaded.

"Like what?" Amusement sparkled in his eyes.

"I don't know. You're a mechanical engineer. You must be able to do something."

"This isn't the movies, Kika. I'm not going to climb out of this cage and do an Eddie Murphy number on the spokes," he said dryly.

"I didn't expect you to," she snapped back.

"Good."

She closed her eyes and took a deep breath.

"You're not going to lose it on me, are you?"

She opened her eyes and looked at him. "I don't know. I don't like heights," she admitted, her palms growing moister by the minute.

"We're only about twenty feet off the ground."

"Twenty too many," she grumbled.

"Nothing's going to happen to you. There are safety features on this contraption."

"I don't care. I don't want to be here." She could feel her self-control slipping away.

"Well, it's a little late to decide that."

Panic threatened to turn her into a simpering idiot. "Ooh, what am I gonna do?"

He slipped his arm around her and gently pulled her closer to him and Melody. "You're going to be okay," he told her in a voice she suspected he usually reserved for his daughter.

Kika's eyes met his. In them she saw comfort and something else, an emotion any woman would recognize in a man's eyes. She shivered, not because she was stranded in the air but because his hand was moving ever so slowly across her shoulder, producing delightful little tremors inside her.

For several moments they stared at each other, neither one saying a word. It was Melody who broke the silence, making a sound that reminded both of them they weren't alone.

Kika looked down at the toddler and saw that she was fingering the purple ribbon tied around the bear's neck.

"Do you like my bear?" Kika pushed the stuffed animal closer to her.

For an answer, Melody put a finger in her mouth and shyly draped her arm across her eyes. The gesture didn't deter Kika.

"Here. Why don't you hold it?" she suggested, placing the bear on Melody's lap.

For her efforts, Kika was rewarded with a smile. It was a grin that touched a place deep inside of her. Normally she felt ill at ease with children, but this little girl was an exception.

As the toddler hugged the plush white bear, Kika asked, "Do you like him?"

This time Melody's response was a nod.

"Maybe you'd like to keep him," Kika offered, which brought a disapproving look to Nick's face.

"That's not necessary," he told her.

"I know it isn't, but I'd like to give it to her if she wants it."

"Why?"

"Why not?" Kika countered.

"I'm not changing my mind about the audition simply because you give my daughter a present," Nick warned her.

Gone was the gentleness he had shown her only moments before. He removed his arm from the back of the seat, and Kika had no doubt that had there been room, he would have put even more distance between them.

"There are no strings attached to the gift, Mr. Miller," she said stiffly.

"Are you sure?"

"Yes."

There was another jerk, and the Ferris wheel started up, went about six feet, then stopped again.

This time the car Kika and Nick rode in came to a halt at the top. Kika's eyes once more met Nick's.

"Are you all right?"

"I'm fine," she said through clenched teeth. It was then that Kika realized she had hold of his arm and was digging her fingernails into his flesh. When she looked at the little girl sitting calmly beside her, she felt ridiculous. Yet she couldn't help it. She hated heights.

"I'm sorry," she said, removing her fingers from his forearm. She shifted ever so cautiously, avoiding looking anywhere but at him.

He shrugged. "It's okay."

She clasped her hands together in her lap to still the trembling. Seeing her obvious uneasiness, he once again slid his arm around her. "You have to try to relax, Kika."

"I am relaxed," she lied.

He didn't contradict her. "Good, because it looks like we're going to be here for a while."

"I'm fine," she told him, and realized it was the truth. Having his arm around her made her feel safe. The warmth of his touch gave her a sense of trust. Nothing would happen as long as he was with her.

His gaze was intense as he said, "I believe you are."

"I am. Just don't rock this thing, okay?" she told him, forcing a smile she wasn't feeling.

"I wouldn't think of it." He continued to stare at her until Melody fidgeted beside him. When she climbed onto his lap, he slid his right arm around her waist.

Being so close to Nick and his daughter brought a lump to Kika's throat. When Melody gazed up at her father with innocent adoration in her green eyes, Kika's chest tightened. She should have had a little girl of her own looking at her with the same innocence.

"Are you sure you're okay?" Nick asked gently.

Kika met his probing gaze. "Yeah. I think we should keep talking though."

"All right. Tell me about your family."

"There's not much to tell. I live in Eagan, which is a suburb of the Twin Cities. As you can guess, my family is Italian. I have three older brothers, no sisters, a mom and a dad—you know, the usual."

"Ever been married?"

She chuckled. "Uh-uh."

"Why is that a funny question?"

"It's not a funny question if you're my parents."

"But to you it is?"

"Let's just say that if I put all the men I've dated in a room with you for twenty-four hours, you'd understand."

"So you haven't met Mr. Right?"

"If I have, he hasn't given me any reason to believe he is," she replied. "Anyway, it doesn't matter. I'm not looking for him."

"What about your work? Do you like being a casting director?"

"You mean do I like bullying people into doing something they don't want to do?"

He winced. "I didn't say that."

"No, but you're thinking it. Actually, Nick, you're going to find this hard to believe, but people usually try to persuade me that they're right for a part."

"Melody isn't like most children, Kika."

"No, she's not," Kika agreed, glancing down at the redheaded child. "There's something special about her—I saw it that first time I watched Glenna's video.''

"She looks like her mother."

The tone of his voice made Kika wonder if he didn't regret the fact that his daughter looked like his wife.

"Was she a redhead?"

"Actually, she was a brunette like Cece, but she had a definite hint of auburn in her hair. Annabelle said she had red curls as a child."

"I always thought that hair color was a trait passed down on the paternal side of the family," Kika remarked.

"There aren't many redheaded Millers. I figure it must have been the combination of genes responsible for the kids."

"They're fortunate. Lots of people would love to have such a glorious color," she said, admiring Melody's soft ringlets.

"Women maybe, but Zach and Patrick get a little annoyed with the attention it draws. Neither one understands why they're called redheads when they say their hair isn't technically red."

"They have a point," she agreed. "I can tell you something. There's a great demand in modeling for children with their coloring."

The mention of her profession put the tension back in their conversation. After several moments of silence, she said, "You know, you and I have something in common."

He raised one eyebrow. "And what would that be?"

"Neither one of us has been in Tyler very long."

He looked at her curiously. "I'm surprised you're here now. I thought you would have spent the holiday with your family."

"I usually do, but this year I wanted to experience the Fourth of July celebration in a small town."

"It's rather low-key for someone who's in the entertainment industry, isn't it?"

"Refreshingly so," she agreed, refusing to hear the hint of sarcasm in his tone. "There's something about not having to lock your car doors every time you stop at a shop that renews your faith in humanity."

"I know what you mean. I think it's going to take me a while to get used to the idea that the boys can bike to the park by themselves. When you live in a big city you get so used to the threat of violence you forget that there are places like Tyler."

"Is that why you moved here? So your children would have a safer place to live?"

"It was definitely a consideration," he admitted, unsure whether he should tell her the true reason for the move. Did he want her to know that he was running away from the past with Beth? That he could no longer live in what she had called their own little piece of paradise?

"I would imagine it's nice for them to be close to their grandmother, too."

"And the rest of the Scanlons," he said, enjoying the way she fit in the curve of his arm. It felt good to hold her. Too good, he thought as she clung to him in much the same way as Melody.

Protective instincts combined with another emotion to make him acutely aware of the fact that he held a very sexy woman in his arms.

"I like Cece. She was very sweet today when I fainted."

The innocence in Kika's tone was in direct contrast to the image she projected. Either she was refreshingly naive or else she was making a fool of him. Uncertainty put an edge to his words. "She certainly helped you make a quick recovery."

"What's that supposed to mean?" Kika straightened and leaned away from him, apparently forgetting her fear of heights.

"It was rather convenient that you fainted where you did," he said wryly.

Indignation caused her shoulders to stiffen. "Are you suggesting that I pretended to faint in order to get your attention?"

"Now why would I think a thing like that?" he asked with mock innocence.

"Yes, why would you?" she demanded.

"Maybe because you've been trying to get my attention ever since your attempt to hit on me at the airport failed."

"My attempt to hit on you?"

He chuckled sarcastically. "Do you always pack your lacy undergarments at the top of your suitcase?"

"I can't believe this! You think I was hitting on you?"

"Do you know what a white Corsica looks like?" he asked in a falsetto voice that mocked hers.

"I was being friendly."

"And is that why you bought a ticket for the Ferris wheel when you have a fear of heights? Because you were being 'friendly'?"

"Yes!" she declared vehemently.

Once more the Ferris wheel regained power, only to lose it after a few seconds. As the conveyance jerked to a halt, Kika pounded her hands on the metal safety bar. "When is it going to stop doing this?" she cried in frustration.

Melody let out a squeal as the bear slid off her lap. Nick grabbed it, but instead of giving it back to her, he shoved it at Kika. Melody whined in protest.

"I gave it to her." Kika let the little girl have the bear. Melody clutched it to her bosom as if it were a beloved keepsake.

Once again the Ferris wheel began to move, and this time it continued its rotation. After only a couple of spins, the attendant began to unload passengers. When they were told to raise a hand if they wanted to be let off, both Nick's and Kika's arms shot up.

As Kika scrambled out of the seat, Nick noticed that the fear she'd held in check while they were stuck at the top was now pushing to the surface. She looked extremely fragile as she made her way to the exit. Immediately he regretted arguing with her. Just because she was sexy and he was attracted to her didn't mean he had to act like such an idiot. Had he really accused her of trying to pick him up? Right now she looked as though she couldn't get away from him fast enough.

The stuffed bear was nearly as big as Melody, which made movement for the two of them difficult. Nick lifted the toddler and the cumbersome toy animal into his arms and stumbled toward the exit. Had it not been for Zachary and Patrick still riding the Ferris wheel, he would have been tempted to follow

Kika and apologize, but he needed to make sure his sons were safely on the ground first.

To his surprise, Kika stopped of her own accord. When Zachary called out to her, catching her attention, she waved up at the boys, who shouted with glee. Then she turned to Nick and said, "At least someone's having fun."

Nick felt a pang of guilt. She had done everything in her power not to let her fear get the better of her at the top of the Ferris wheel, yet he had acted like a jerk. And all because he was attracted to her. As he watched her move away, he saw one of the men from the softball teams walk up to her, put his arm around her shoulder and lead her toward the food concessions.

"There you are." Annabelle's voice sounded over Nick's shoulder. "I've been looking for you and the boys. Where on earth did you get that thing?" she asked, looking at the white bear as if it were a postal patron wanting to buy a stamp at closing time.

Nick was saved from having to answer by the appearance of Zachary and Patrick, who came rushing out of the exit gate, boasting of their misadventure.

"Slow down and speak one at a time," Annabelle commanded.

"It was so cool, Grandma."

"We were stuck at the top!"

Nick only half listened to the boys telling of their experience on the stalled amusement ride. His eyes were on Kika and the muscular athlete, who seemed to be getting friendlier by the minute. When they stopped at the ice cream booth, Nick felt an odd little pang of envy when the softball player bought her a cone. Nick could have been the one to buy her a treat.

"Come. We're going to get ice cream," he heard Annabelle state in her commanding voice.

"Maybe we should wait a bit," Nick said, not wanting to follow Kika to the concession stand. His suggestion was met with a chorus of groans. "Don't you want to go on some more rides?" he asked his sons.

When they assured him that all they wanted at the moment was ice cream, he had no choice but to give in. "All right. We'll go."

Just great, Nick thought. All he needed was to have his three kids and his mother-in-law in tow when he saw Kika Mancini again. Not that it would matter. She was interested in his daughter, not him.

For a brief time on the Ferris wheel he had started to think of her as a woman, not a talent scout. When she was sitting close to him it seemed a natural thing to do. Now that he had both feet back on the ground he realized that to think of Kika Mancini at all could only invite trouble.

"WHAT FLAVOR? Chocolate or vanilla?" Nick asked his children as he pulled his wallet from his pocket.

"Make sure you get the yogurt. It's better for them," Annabelle told him as he stepped up to the counter.

Overhearing his grandmother, Patrick tugged on Nick's pant leg, "Dad, I don't like yogurt. I want ice cream."

"Two chocolate, one vanilla ice cream and one vanilla yogurt," Nick told the young woman taking his order.

"Do you realize how much fat there is in that ice cream?" Annabelle asked in her loud voice.

"I don't think one scoop is going to clog their arteries for life," he murmured, hoping that Kika Mancini wasn't overhearing their conversation. She and the ball player sat on a bench only a few yards away, a fact that was much more disturbing to Nick than his mother-in-law's nutritional advice.

"The yogurt is produced locally—by Britt Marshack," Annabelle told him. "And it's made from low-fat goat's milk."

"The whole town is surrounded by dairy farms," he retorted.

Annabelle pursed her lips as she whipped several napkins from the metal holder on the counter. She steered the boys over to a park bench and handed them their cones with the warning they were not to get any ice cream on their clothes.

"Aren't you having one?" Annabelle asked as Nick lifted Melody onto the bench.

"I'll help Melody with hers." He plopped the bear down between him and his daughter.

"You never did say how she got that." Annabelle's attitude toward the stuffed animal obviously hadn't changed.

"Did you win it, Dad?" Zachary asked curiously.

Aware of the fact that Kika sat within hearing distance, he said, "No, Kika Mancini gave it to Melody when we were stuck at the top of the Ferris wheel."

Annabelle nearly choked on her vanilla yogurt. "You were on the Ferris wheel with her?"

Nick deliberately misunderstood her and said, "Melody's old enough to go on a few amusement rides. She likes them, don't you, Mel?'' He ruffled his daughter's curls.

Annabelle passed him a napkin. "She has ice cream on her ear."

Nick could see where his daughter had grabbed at the cone with her fingers, then touched her head, leaving a trail of chocolate. She looked endearingly sweet.

"Is she trying to bribe you?" Annabelle asked.

"Who?"

"Ms. Mancini."

He shrugged. "It doesn't matter. It's not going to work." He said the words loud enough so that Kika could hear. In fact, he was certain that she had heard, for she rose to her feet and walked toward them.

"Hello again," she said, sounding as if she had forgotten that their last conversation had ended on less-than-friendly terms. She had an energy about her that wasn't all that different from the exuberance his children displayed, Nick decided.

"Kika, wasn't that cool, getting stuck on the Ferris wheel?" Zachary asked.

"It was pretty neat, Zach." Her eyes dared Nick to contradict her statement.

So she was going to pretend that nothing had happened. It was fine with him.

"Did you enjoy the ice cream?" Nick asked.

"Actually, I had the yogurt," Kika told him. "It was delicious."

That brought a look of triumph to Annabelle's face. She took the opportunity to explain to Kika how Britt Marshack had started Yes! Yogurt when her dairy farm was on the brink of financial disaster.

Not wanting to waste time listening to adults talk while there was so much activity at the carnival, Zach asked, "Can we go watch The Rocket? We'll be right over there, where you can see us." He pointed to a spot not more than a hundred feet away.

"You better finish your ice cream first," Annabelle answered.

"If you wait just a few minutes, I'll take you as soon as Melody's finished," Nick told his son.

"I can take them," Kika offered. "I like watching The Rocket tumble, too."

"Can she, Dad?" Zachary's eyes lit up.

Had Annabelle's expression not been so disapproving Nick might have told the boys to wait. Despite his intent to stay away from the beautiful talent scout he found himself saying to her, "Are you sure you don't mind?"

"No, I'd be happy to take them." She placed a hand on each of their shoulders and said, "Steer me in the right direction, boys."

"They're going to get ice cream all over their clothes," Annabelle warned as the three of them walked away.

"It'll wash out," Nick answered.

"I wouldn't leave them with her too long. Before you know it she'll be putting ideas in their heads and they'll be telling you they want to be in movies," Annabelle cautioned.

That was the last thing on Nick's mind. Right now he needed to find a way to deal with the feelings he experienced every time Kika Mancini flashed those big brown eyes in his direction.

As he watched his sons go off with the casting director there was only one thought running through his head. He wished he were the one she had her arm around.

CHAPTER SIX

"DAD, CAN I GO on The Rocket?"

Nick ignored Zachary's request. Ever since he had found the boys standing beside Kika like a couple of cherubs, their hands linked with hers, he had been preoccupied with one thought—how perfectly at ease she was with them. It was a disturbing concept. Someone who disliked children had no business pretending she wanted to be with them.

Zachary repeated his request.

"I'm going to go, too," Patrick boasted, only to have his brother squash his enthusiasm.

"You're too little. See?" Zach pointed to a wooden cutout of a cartoon character next to the entrance. "It says if you don't reach that mark you can't ride without an adult."

"Zach's right. You can't ride without me and I have to stay with Melody," Nick told his son.

"I could take the boys," Kika offered. "That is, if you think the three of us could fit in one seat?"

"You want to go with us?" Zachary's eyes lit up. "Can she, Dad? Please?"

Nick propped his free hand—the one that wasn't holding on to Melody—on his waist and faced Kika. "I thought you hated heights."

"After what happened on the Ferris wheel, I'm cured." She used her hands to emphasize her words.

Nick had a pretty darn good idea that she was lying. What was she up to, anyway? Whatever it was, he wasn't going to play into her hands.

"It's not a good idea. You boys have been on enough rides for one day," Nick told his sons, annoyed that Kika was making him look like the heavy.

"But Dad, we've only been on the kiddie rides. The Rocket's the coolest ride here. All my friends have been on it," Zachary pleaded.

Nick was about to say no for the second time when Kika intervened on the boys' behalf. "I really don't mind taking them. Of course, if you'd rather go, I could stay down here with Melody."

So that was it. She wanted him to go so she could stay on the ground with his daughter. She still hadn't given up on the idea of Melody being in that commercial.

Nick glared at her. It would serve her right if he let her go on The Rocket. Maybe she needed to come unglued in front of his sons so they would quit gazing at her as if she were their fairy godmother.

Yet something inside him refused to let him give in to the temptation. Instead he said, "I'd like to say yes, but Grandma's waiting for us. The fireworks are going to start in a few minutes."

"But look how short the line is." Zachary continued to plead his case. "If we went now we'd get right on."

"I'll buy the tickets—my treat," Kika offered in what was clearly a challenge.

"Please say yes, Dad!" both boys begged. "Please!"

Nick knew he had lost. "All right, but this is your last ride."

Kika gave him a smug grin as she pranced past him to the ticket kiosk. Instead of being angry, he found himself wanting to pull her into his arms and kiss her. He quickly pushed that thought out of his head.

A few minutes later she flashed three tickets under his nose. "Who's going? You or me?"

"I'll go," he said, taking the tickets from her. Reluctantly, he relinquished Melody's hand and gave Kika the white bear as well. As he climbed on board The Rocket, he tried not to notice how attractive Kika looked standing beside his daughter. It was useless. There was something about her that drew his attention.

"Our insides are going to get all shook up," Patrick proclaimed as they climbed into the narrow confines of The Rocket's seat.

Nick knew that his insides were already that way simply from being in the presence of one bouncy, vivacious blonde. He hoped that the tumbling and turning of The Rocket would toss his emotions into some sort of order, the way they had been before he had met her.

It didn't happen. As soon as the ride was over and all three of them were back on the ground, Zachary asked, "Can Kika watch the fireworks with us?"

"I'm sure she has other things she wants to do," Nick answered smoothly, stuffing the bear under his arm as he grabbed Melody by the hand.

"As a matter of fact, I don't. I would love to come watch the fireworks. But if you don't have room for me?" Kika gave him a wide-eyed, innocent look that put an extra kick in his heartbeat. She was flirting with him again and he liked it.

"Grandma brought two blankets and her lawn chair," Zachary interjected.

Nick could imagine the look on Annabelle's face if he were to bring Kika Mancini back with him. It didn't matter. He wanted her to come along. "I guess that means we have plenty of room."

"Great. I'd love to join you," she said, giving all of them a big smile.

Just as Nick suspected, Annabelle was not delighted to see Kika. Fortunately, Zachary and Patrick launched into a detailed account of their trip on The Rocket, preventing their grandmother from saying anything but a polite hello. Nick wondered if Kika thought Annabelle was deliberately ignoring her.

He had a difficult time being angry with the older woman. He didn't believe her attitude was intentional. She was just so busy barking out orders to her grandchildren to pull on sweatshirts and spread out the blanket that she had no time to socialize with Kika.

The sun had disappeared, taking with it the warmth that had motivated people to dress in shorts for the parade. With the night came a coolness that surprised Nick. He wondered if Kika was chilly in her white shorts.

His unasked question was answered moments later when she said, "I wonder if I should go back to my car and get my jacket."

Nick was relieved to hear Annabelle say, "There's an extra lap robe behind Patrick."

Nick reached around his son and grabbed the red plaid woolen blanket. He shook it open, then draped it over Kika's shoulders.

"What about you? Aren't you cold?" she asked.

Cold? All he had to do was catch a glimpse of her bare legs and his blood ran hot. "I'm okay."

"Maybe the kids want to share this?" Kika suggested, spreading her arms in a gesture that invited them to come sit beside her. Neither of the boys wanted to sit still. They had discovered a couple of friends from Adventure Club and were running around playing tag. Melody looked at Kika, but didn't move toward her.

"Are you cold?" Nick asked his daughter.

She shook her head. Then she gave Kika the bear, which Kika pulled into the crook of her arm and cuddled beneath the blanket.

"Are you sure you don't want to sit beside him?" Kika asked the little girl, but she shyly shook her head.

"Have you given him a name yet?" Kika asked.

Again she shook her head, but with a finger in her mouth, she inched closer. Finally she sat down on the blanket, a few feet away.

Just when it looked as if she might move closer to Kika, a large explosion split the air. The first of the fireworks had been ignited. Startled, Melody looked from her father to Kika, then burst into tears. Kika opened her arms, but Melody ran toward her grandmother.

Annabelle scooped her up, cuddling her in a tender embrace. She rocked her in her lap, speaking words of comfort in her ear. Kika could only look on with a sense of rejection. How foolish she had been to think anything had changed. She didn't have what it took to be a mother.

The first burst of color brought the boys diving onto the blanket. They spoke nearly nonstop to Kika, asking her which colors she liked best and comparing the different patterns the fireworks left in the sky.

But it wasn't the Miller boys' attention she wanted. It was the affection of one small, two-year-old girl who, instead of running to Kika's arms for comfort, had bolted like a scared rabbit.

Kika forced a brightness to her voice that she wasn't feeling. She couldn't think about what had happened with Melody Miller. Kika wasn't supposed to be the object of the little girl's affection. She couldn't be. There was no room in her heart for that kind of feeling.

As the fireworks lit the nighttime sky, she pretended to be having a great time. She oohed and aahed with the boys and ignored the man to her left and the little girl to her right, two people who in a very short time had succeeded in unwinding her heartstrings.

Spending the day with the Millers, Kika had come dangerously close to forgetting the reason she was in Tyler. She needed to remind herself that she wasn't one of the crowd. She was an outsider. It would be best if she stayed close to Annabelle Scanlon so she didn't forget that.

She had a goal—to get Fancy's Baby. She only hoped that Fancy's Baby didn't get her heart.

KIKA WASN'T the only one feeling a bit put out that Melody had chosen her grandmother's arms for comfort. As the last of the fireworks lit the sky, Nick wondered why his daughter wasn't lying against his chest.

Normally, he would have gone over to Annabelle and lifted the little girl out of her arms. However, he

wasn't sure Melody wouldn't have cried if he had, and
it there was one thing he didn't need Kika Mancini to
see it was his less-than-perfect relationship with his
daughter.

So at the end of the colorful display, instead of
taking care of Melody, he took charge of folding the
blankets and gathering up the supplies Annabelle had
brought. As they started the walk home, he realized
Kika would be going to her car in the dark.

"Where are you parked?" he asked.

She looked around a moment in confusion. "I
think I'm thataway," she answered, stabbing at the
air with a finger.

"If you wait, I'll make sure you find your car. But
first I have to take the kids home," he told her.

Patrick, who had become very sleepy all of a sudden, said, "Do we have to walk all the way home? I'm
tired."

Seeing the boys dragging their feet, Annabelle said,
"Why don't I take them back to my house? It's
closer."

"Maybe that would be best. I can pick them up after I help Kika find her car. Is that all right with you
guys?" Nick asked his sons.

To his surprise, there were no objections to his
plan. So while Annabelle walked off with Melody and
the boys, he went with Kika, two folded blankets in
one arm, a lawn chair under the other.

"Is it a rental car?" Nick asked as they crossed
Main Street.

"Umm-hmm. Another Corsica—only this one's
blue."

He chuckled. "Probably the same one I had last
week."

"You're not driving a rental car?"

"No, I bought a new one. Just got it yesterday."

She motioned for him to take a right at the next corner. They found the Corsica parked next to the curb.

"Do you want me to give you a ride to Annabelle's?" she asked, leaning against the door in a rather seductive pose.

The thought of being in the car with her was a tempting one for Nick. The longer he was in her company, the more he wanted to forget that she was not the kind of woman he should find attractive.

"Is that an invitation?"

"Yes. I'm inviting you to accept my offer of a ride. Nothing more, nothing less."

"I see."

"So would you like a ride or not?"

What he wanted was to take her to his home, where they could be alone together.

He quickly squelched those thoughts. He had three kids waiting to be picked up at his mother-in-law's house.

"I'll walk, thanks," he said coolly.

"Fine. See ya." She went to pull the door open, only to discover it was locked. She patted the pockets of her shorts, then turned around with a groan. "I don't have the keys. I remember putting them in my pocket...." She bent over to peer through the glass. "Oh, no."

"They're inside?"

She nodded miserably. "On the seat. I must have missed my pocket."

No surprise, Nick thought. Judging by the size of her shorts, he guessed the pockets had to be pretty small. "I thought you said one of the nice things about being in Tyler was that you didn't have to lock your car."

"It is. I must have done it automatically. It's so second nature to me." She thrust her fists on her hips. "Now what am I going to do?"

Nick decided that if he were smart he'd escort her to the police station and let the authorities help her with her problem. "We can probably figure out a way to get inside," he found himself saying.

"We?"

"I'll help you. I am a mechanical engineer."

"I know, but this isn't the movies and you're not Eddie Murphy," she reminded him, a sly grin spreading across her face.

Damn. Did she always have to have such a sexy glint in her eyes when she talked to him? "No, but this is a challenge no tool man worth his wrenches would turn down."

"So what do you suggest we do? I know the old wire coat hanger trick doesn't work on these new cars."

"I can probably find something in my tool chest to help you out."

"And just where is this tool chest?"

"At my house. It's only about four blocks from here if you want to walk with me." When she didn't respond right away, he added, "Or we could go back to the carnival and hope to find some help."

"There must be a service station in town."

"There's Carl's Garage, across from Gates Department Store. I'm not sure he'd be open this late, though."

"You're probably right. Maybe we should go to your place," she suggested.

Nick shrugged. "Sure." As they crossed the street, he realized that he hadn't mentioned the other alternative—about getting someone from the police department to open the door.

But then he wouldn't have an excuse to spend more time with Kika Mancini. And that was what he wanted to do. He was starting to enjoy the sparks that flew between the two of them.

As they walked the short distance to his house, he deliberately kept silent, knowing she was not the type to stay speechless for long. She soon proved he was right.

"Zachary says that you're good at fixing things."

"Some things," he conceded. "So what else did my son tell you?"

"That you're starting a new job on Monday in Milwaukee and that you'll be working four ten-hour days, which means on Fridays you'll be able to do fun things."

"That's the plan."

"You sound as if you have reservations that it'll work."

"It's been a struggle to fit fun things into the schedule ever since my wife died," he admitted.

"How long ago was that?" she asked gently.

"Almost two years."

"But Melody's only..." She trailed off.

"Twenty-two months. My wife died in childbirth."

Kika reached out a hand and placed it on his arm. "I'm sorry. It must have been very painful for you and the boys."

"We've adjusted," he told her, although he knew it wasn't entirely true. "Melody's the one I worry about."

"She's never known a mother's love. No wonder..." Again Kika didn't finish her sentence.

"No wonder what?" he asked impatiently. "She doesn't talk?"

Kika stopped to face him. "That's not what I was going to say."

"Isn't it? If you're thinking that I'm so caught up in my grief I can't give Melody the attention she needs, you're wrong."

She thrust her fists on her hips once again. "I don't need you to tell me what I'm thinking, Nick Miller. For your information, I was going to say no wonder she rushes to her grandmother's arms when she needs comforting."

Even though it was dark, Nick could see the sparkle in Kika's eyes. He sensed a genuine compassion in her, which made him want to talk about his family—something he normally didn't do with strangers.

"I'm sorry." They started walking again. "You're right. Since Melody's been in Tyler she's become quite attached to her grandmother."

"Does that bother you?"

"No." Again it wasn't the complete truth. "She needs a woman in her life. So do the boys."

"And what about you?"

"I haven't given it much thought." Again he wasn't quite honest.

"Maybe you should."

He couldn't tell if she were being provocative or not. This time he was the one who stopped. "What if

I wanted you to be that woman?'' He couldn't believe he had uttered the words.

Neither could she, by the look on her face. Her voice was husky when she said, ''Be careful what you wish for, Nick. You just might get it.''

Her eyes held his, challenging him to make a move. He hesitated only for a second before pulling her into his arms. Gently, he brushed her mouth with his. During the brief contact, he had a tantalizing hint of a passion waiting to be uncovered.

To his surprise, she kissed him back. She pressed her lips against his, coaxing them into a response that invited intimacy. He accepted the invitation, slipping his tongue into her mouth. A shudder of pleasure ran through him as the kiss deepened, her arms sliding upward over his shoulders to cling to the back of his neck. Nick could feel himself drowning in sensations, as needs he had long denied demanded to be satisfied.

It was the sound of a horn honking that made them pull apart. Two headlights pinned them in their beams. Nick glanced around and realized they were standing at the entrance of a driveway, where someone wanted to park a car. They quickly scrambled out of the way.

Kika giggled. ''Do you know that woman?''

''Fortunately, I don't.'' He liked the way Kika's hand felt in his and decided to keep it there as they continued down the residential street.

They walked in silence until they reached the two-story house that was beginning to look familiar to Nick. ''Why don't you wait on the swing and I'll go get what I need from the garage?'' he suggested, gesturing for her to take a seat on the porch.

He slipped into the garage through the service door, flipping a switch as he entered. Although he had sold all the furnishings of their California home, Nick had kept his tools. Fortunately, Mr. Watson had been a handyman. Built-in cabinets and shelves lined the walls of the garage. One of the first tasks Nick had accomplished when he had moved into the house was to unpack his tools and put them away.

He pulled open a drawer on the workbench and found a long, narrow strip of metal. Next he grabbed a flashlight, then turned off the garage light and went back outside. Gently swaying back and forth on the porch swing, Kika looked even more attractive than she had earlier that evening. She also looked chilled.

"Would you like to borrow my jacket?" he asked, slipping his arms out of the navy-blue windbreaker.

"Thanks." She took it from him and slipped it on. "What's that?" she asked, gesturing to the metal strip in his hand.

"This is your key. At least, with any luck it will be. Why don't you wait here and I'll bring my car around to the front?"

He went back into the garage and got his brand-new red Mustang convertible. As he pulled up in front of the house, she came hurrying down the sidewalk.

"Nice car," she said with a grin as she slid inside. "I never expected you would drive a convertible."

"What kind of a car did you think I would have?"

"I don't know. A minivan or a station wagon, I guess."

"Why? Because you think I don't know how to have fun?"

"No, because you're a father with three kids."

"So?" The tires squealed as he pulled away from the curb. He felt like a teenager trying to show off in front of his girl.

"This is really fun," Kika exclaimed, staring up at the starry sky. "Do you know, I've never been in a convertible with its top down at night?"

"Now that I find hard to believe."

"It's true. I grew up with a father who continually reminded me that convertibles weren't practical in a climate where you need heat nine months of the year. I suppose you cruised Sunset Boulevard with all the other Hollywood teens, right?"

"Don't I wish. My father thought convertibles weren't practical, period. Maybe that's why I have one now. I always wanted one as a kid."

The ride was over much too soon for Nick. By the time they reached her car, her hair was windblown and her eyes were sparkling. Never had she looked more beautiful.

"Why don't you hold the flashlight and I'll see what I can do," he told her, handing her the lantern.

Nick worked the long strip of metal between the rubber edging and the glass window. It wasn't long before he could reach the automatic lock button and the door opened.

"You did it!" Kika exclaimed in relief. "You are good at fixing things, aren't you?"

"As I said, some things." He didn't want to tell her that inanimate objects were a piece of cake compared to human emotions.

Kika swung the car door open and slid inside. "Look. Here they are." She held up the car keys for his inspection. "Thank you for your help."

"You're welcome," he answered, leaning over her. His mouth still tingled from the kisses they had shared. The mere thought was enough to send his blood pounding through his veins.

"You're going to have to let me think of a way to repay you," she told him. "Why don't you come to Timberlake Lodge for dinner tomorrow night?"

"It's not necessary," he answered, ignoring the protest his hormones made at his declaration.

"But I want to do it," she insisted.

It was a tempting offer. Mentally, he debated whether he should accept. If he went, he would send her a signal that he was attracted to her. The smart move would be to refuse. Unfortunately, he didn't want to do the smart thing.

"All right. Dinner it is."

"Seven okay?"

"Seven's fine."

"Good." She reached for the door. Reluctantly, he stepped aside so she could shut it. She rolled down the window. "You're a nice man, Nick Miller. Good night."

She had pulled away from the curb and was about halfway down the block when she stepped on her brakes, lighting up the rear end of the car as she backed up. She stopped in the middle of the street, got out and came running toward him.

"I almost forgot this," she said, pulling off his jacket. "Thanks for loaning it to me." She handed it to him.

Just as quickly, she returned to her car and drove away. Nick slid his arms into the sleeves of the nylon windbreaker. It was still warm from her body and he could smell the faint aroma of wildflowers.

A wave of longing shot through him. As he drove the short distance to Annabelle's, all he could think about was how good Kika had felt in his arms. It had been so long since those familiar stirrings of desire had coursed through him. They reminded him of what he used to have with Beth.

A feeling of guilt washed over him. His love for Beth had been so passionate. Not once in their thirteen years of marriage had he ever desired another woman. Now he did and the feeling was unsettling.

He didn't want to be attracted to Kika Mancini. She was just the opposite of what he needed—the exact opposite of Beth. Something his mother-in-law reminded him of when he arrived at her house.

"What took you so long?" Annabelle demanded the minute he stepped inside.

"Kika had locked her keys inside the car. I had to help her get the door open," Nick answered.

"Why would she lock her car in Tyler? Surely she must know this isn't like the city. You can trust the people here." Annabelle clicked her tongue. "That's the problem with city folks. They're so suspicious of everything."

Nick wanted to remind her that he was a city person, too, and so had Beth been for the last thirteen years of her life. Somehow it didn't seem worth mentioning.

"She didn't do it intentionally."

"I wouldn't be too sure of that. While you were helping her out, she didn't just happen to try to convince you to let Melody audition?"

"No, we didn't talk about Melody."

"Thank goodness. Did you see the way Melody ran from her? It doesn't surprise me. The woman looks uncomfortable around children.'' She harrumphed. ''No wonder she can't find Fancy's Baby.''

Again Nick came to her defense. ''The boys seem to like her.''

''That's because she's throwing around all those showbiz names, trying to impress people.''

Nick decided it was better not to discuss Kika Mancini with his mother-in-law, especially after what had happened this evening. Thank goodness Annabelle hadn't seen them kissing.

''Dad, can we go home now?'' Zachary asked, his voice weary as he trudged into the kitchen.

''Sure. Where's Melody?''

''She fell asleep on my bed,'' Annabelle answered. ''She can stay with me tonight if you like.''

Nick didn't like the idea. Ever since he had arrived in Tyler he felt as if his daughter preferred the company of her grandmother over his. He tried to be objective about the situation. After all, he was the one who wanted Melody to have a woman's influence in her life. But it still bothered him.

''Don't you have to work in the morning?'' Nick asked his mother-in-law.

''Yes, but I can bring her by on my way to the post office. Don't worry. It's no problem.''

Maybe for her it wasn't, but for Nick it was. How could he not worry about his daughter? Melody was a miniature of the woman he had loved and lost. Now he had this awful feeling that his daughter was slowly slipping away from him, that she would grow up without needing him in her life.

He knew it was an irrational fear. She was his daughter, and all he had to do was be there for her. Yet in the nearly two years since Beth's death, that had been a difficult assignment. Now Annabelle seemed to be able to reach her in a way he hadn't been able to thus far, convincing him that it wasn't his daughter who had the problem, but him.

Reluctantly, he left Melody to spend the night with Annabelle. Zachary and Patrick chose to go home with him.

"I'm glad you didn't make us sleep over at Grandma's," Zachary told his father when they were in the car.

"Me, too," Patrick chipped in, adding to Nick's uneasiness.

"Why is that?" Nick asked, even though he wasn't sure he wanted to know the answer.

"I like my new bed better than the one at Grandma's. Hers is hard," Zachary said, which made Nick a little less uncomfortable.

"And she makes us eat all kinds of yucky stuff," Patrick added. "Except Melody doesn't have to. I think Grandma likes her better cuz she's a girl."

"Plus she's a baby. Grown-ups always treat babies as if they're something special," Zachary said astutely.

"Melody is special, don't you think?" Nick asked.

"Grandma says she's just like Mom, but I saw pictures of Mom when she was a baby and she didn't look like Melody at all," Zachary told his father.

Nick felt the familiar emptiness that always came over him when one of his sons mentioned Beth. He figured it was a blessing that children were resilient. Their loss was as great as his, yet they had managed to leave their sorrow behind. Something he hadn't quite managed to do yet.

As he pulled up in front of the house, Patrick's excitable chatter diverted his attention.

"Hey, Dad! You forgot to close the garage door," the six-year-old announced.

Nick had a sinking feeling in the pit of his stomach. The light was off inside the garage, but the door was wide open. He had been so preoccupied with impressing Kika Mancini with his wheels that he hadn't even realized that he hadn't shut the garage door.

"I hope nobody stole our bikes!" Zachary scrambled out of the car as soon as it came to a stop.

A quick inventory of the garage assured all three of them that everything was in the same place it had been earlier that day. Three mountain bikes were parked against the far wall. Nick's tools still hung from hooks and lined the shelves of the workbench. He breathed a sigh of relief.

"We can go inside now. Nothing's missing." He herded his sons out of the garage.

"It's a good thing we moved to Tyler, huh, Dad?" Zachary said as they climbed the porch steps to the house.

"You're right, Zach. It's a good thing," Nick agreed.

As they prepared for bed, Zach said, "It was a great day, wasn't it, Dad?"

"It was pretty good," Nick agreed.

"I loved getting stuck on the Ferris wheel, didn't you?"

"It was fun," Nick answered honestly, then ruffled his son's hair as he said good-night.

Long after the boys had fallen asleep, Nick sat out on the front porch swing, thinking about everything that had happened that day. It had been a special

Fourth of July celebration. For the first time since Beth died, life seemed almost normal. Part of the reason was that he and the kids had spent the holiday with family. The other part had to do with Kika Mancini. As much as he hated to admit it, she had been able to part the clouds that had shaded his emotions.

CHAPTER SEVEN

"WHEW. IT'S HOT today, isn't it?" As she stepped up to the counter in the post office, Tessie Finklebaum dabbed at the tufts of platinum-tinted hair that poked through the center of her sun visor.

Annabelle could tell by the way Tessie's eyes avoided hers that the older woman knew something about somebody. If there was one thing Annabelle had learned in her years as the town's postmistress, it was how to read people's faces. And right now Tessie's flushed cheeks were telling her she had a secret she was dying to share.

"So what brings you out in this heat? You got some good gossip or something?" Annabelle was not one to beat around the bush.

"Oh, no," the woman replied quickly. "I just wanted to get this in the mail." She waved a pink envelope in front of Annabelle. "It's a birthday card for my niece—the one who's teaching in Australia."

Annabelle took the greeting card, eyeing it dubiously as she placed it on the scale. "One dollar air mail."

"I have that here somewhere." Again avoiding Annabelle's eyes, Tessie dug into her black fanny pack for the exact change. She plunked three quarters, two dimes and a nickel down on the counter.

Then she picked up the postage stamp, licked it and slapped it on the envelope.

"There." She gave Annabelle a weak smile. "Now I know it'll get there on time." She zipped her fanny pack shut and looked out at the bright sunshine. "Well, time to go back out into the heat."

She started to turn away, but Annabelle stopped her.

"Not so fast. You're not going anywhere yet."

Tessie was not one to startle easily. She gave the postmistress an innocent look, saying, "I beg your pardon?"

"You're not leaving until you tell me what's making you look like the cat who was asked to clean out the canary cage.... Come on. Out with it," Annabelle demanded when Tessie remained mute. "What's the scoop?"

"Why, Annabelle Scanlon. You ought to know I'm not one to gossip. When I worked for the Barons I had the reputation of being the soul of discretion."

"Yeah, yeah, I know," Annabelle said with a wave of her hand. "But you're not a legal secretary anymore. You retired your discretion along with your steno pad. You're just one of us now and you might as well tell me what it is you know, because I'm going to hear about it sooner or later."

Tessie moved closer to the counter. "I figured you had heard already."

"Heard what?"

Tessie hesitated only a moment before saying, "About your son-in-law and that Hollywood woman."

Annabelle heaved a long sigh and folded her arms across her chest. "I know she's trying to get my granddaughter to be in that commercial, if that's what you're talking about.''

''So that's what's going on?''

Annabelle eyed her suspiciously. ''There's nothing going on.''

''That's not the way it looked to me.''

''Tessie Finklebaum, what are you talking about?''

''I'm talking about your son-in-law and her.''

The postmistress pursed her lips. Because the little blonde had followed Nick around yesterday, folks were now speculating about their relationship. Annabelle had been afraid something like this would happen. ''Tessie, you of all people ought to know that just because a man likes to walk past the bakery to smell the cookies, it doesn't necessarily mean he's going to take one home.''

''But he did take her home. Last night. I saw them with my own two eyes.''

''Yeah, I know. She locked her keys in the car and Nick had to help her get them out.''

Tessie chuckled sarcastically. ''They weren't anywhere near her car when I saw them and what they were doing had nothing to do with unlocking any door.''

''You're talking in riddles. Why don't you just tell me what you saw them doing?'' she snapped impatiently.

There wasn't another customer in the post office, yet Tessie looked around cautiously before saying in a low voice, ''They were kissing.''

''Kissing?'' Annabelle's jaw dropped and the color drained from her cheeks. ''Nick and the Hollywood agent?''

Tessie nodded vigorously. "I was in my car, trying to turn into my driveway, but I couldn't. They were standing smack-dab in the center of the sidewalk."

"You must be mistaken. Are you sure it was Nick?"

"He's renting the old Watson place just down the block from me, isn't he?"

Annabelle nodded. "But it could have been someone else."

"I had the high beams on! Not that it did any good. They didn't even notice me. I had to honk the horn to get them to move."

Now it all made sense, Annabelle realized—Nick's hazy expression when he had come to pick up the boys last night, his defensive attitude toward the casting agent. For once Annabelle was at a loss for words.

"I knew she was with your family at the picnic yesterday but I had no idea there was more to it than that," Tessie added.

"There isn't more to it." Annabelle quickly found her voice. "And I would appreciate you not sharing this information with anyone else until I've had a chance to talk to my son-in-law."

"He was kissing her, Annabelle." The older woman's words carried a warning.

"Sometimes appearances can be deceptive," Annabelle told her. "You won't say anything, will you, Tessie?"

"Of course not. As I said, I'm the soul of discretion." She made a motion as if she were locking her lips shut, then adjusted her sun visor and left the air-conditioned building.

Annabelle half expected that every patron who entered the post office that day would question her about Nick's relationship with Kika. To her relief, not a single one did.

Annabelle wished she could dismiss the subject herself. When she saw her daughter heading toward the bank across the street, she rushed over to the door, stuck her head outside and shouted, "Cece! Come here! Quick!" She waved frantically.

By the time Cece had crossed the street and entered the post office, Annabelle was back behind the counter, pacing.

"Mother, what's wrong?" Cece asked, concern lining her face.

"You're never going to believe what I heard this morning." She glanced at the six-foot-high divider separating the lobby from the work area to make sure no one was listening, then said, "Tessie Finklebaum saw Nick kissing Kika Mancini."

Cece's worry lines were gradually replaced by a smile. "I had a hunch there was something happening between the two of them yesterday. Nick couldn't keep his eyes off her."

Annabelle clicked her tongue. "Is it any wonder? The way she was dressed, she had half the men in Tyler gawking at her."

"She's got a great figure, Mother, and a lovely face. She could have been dressed in coveralls and the men in Tyler would have still gawked at her."

"You sound as if you like her."

"I do. I think she's fun."

"Fun?" Annabelle made another sound of disgust. "I wish she would stay away from Nick."

"Why should she? He is a single man."

"He's a father with three kids!"

"That doesn't mean he can't date."

A horrified look crossed her face. "You think he wants to date her?"

Cece shrugged. "So what if he does?"

"Cece, she's a barracuda!"

Just then the door opened and in walked Brick Bauer, the chief of police. "How's it going, ladies? Did everyone have a good time at the picnic yesterday?"

Annabelle glanced at Cece, who saw the police chief's entrance as her opportunity to leave. "It was great fun, Brick. I'll let my mother fill you in on the details. I have an appointment." And with a wave, she was gone.

Annabelle turned her attention to the man in the uniform, but her thoughts were on one thing and one thing only: she couldn't let Nick make a big mistake.

It was obvious that Cece wasn't going to be any help in preventing that from happening. There was only one thing for Annabelle to do—fight fire with fire.

"Brick, you're just the man I wanted to see. Remember when we talked about fixing Nick up with that friend of yours who lives in Sugar Creek? You know, the schoolteacher who lost her husband last year in that automobile accident?"

"You think he'd be interested?" Brick asked.

"Oh, I'm sure he'd be," Annabelle answered, her mind already racing ahead to ways of getting them together. "Why don't you give her a call?"

EVER SINCE Nick had kissed Kika, she had been unable to get the man off her mind. All she could think about was when she might see him again.

That was why she threw herself into her work the following morning, going ahead with the plans for the audition. With or without Melody Miller, she was going to have a video crew in Tyler to try to find Fancy's Baby.

Since there wasn't a soundstage in the vicinity, she arranged to set up the film crew in the high-school gymnasium for the first round of interviews. Callbacks would have to be conducted in Minneapolis, which was probably a good thing, since Kika knew she was getting dangerously close to becoming emotionally involved with the Miller children. It was something she couldn't allow to happen.

Feeling restless and a bit homesick, she was grateful when her sister-in-law called to see how things were progressing.

"We missed you yesterday," Frannie told her, causing Kika's heartstrings to tighten another turn. Every year the Mancini family spent the Fourth of July at one of Kika's uncles' cabins in northern Minnesota. This was the first time in five years that Kika had missed the get-together. "Frankie was there."

"Then it's probably a good thing I wasn't," Kika told her, although she did regret missing the annual event.

"Tell me what the Fourth was like in Tyler."

Kika recounted incidents of the previous day, barely mentioning Nick's presence. Frannie, however, read between the lines.

"Oh, my gosh! You had a date with that hunk from the video?" She could hardly contain her excitement.

"It wasn't a date, Frannie. His family invited me to eat with them at the picnic, we watched fireworks and he helped me get into my car after I locked the keys inside," Kika explained. She was sitting in a hammock on the balcony of her room at the lodge, the phone propped between her ear and her shoulder.

"Way to go, Kika!"

"It's not what you think."

"And what am I thinking?"

"I can hear your matchmaking motor clicking away."

Frannie gasped in mock indignation. "Just because you're away from home and I think you should make the most of an opportunity to spend time with a gorgeous bachelor does not mean I'm matchmaking."

"There is no opportunity."

"Uh-huh." Frannie did not sound convinced. "So tell me about this mechanical engineer."

"There's nothing to tell," Kika answered, coiling the phone cord around her fingers.

"Well, I already know he's tall, dark and handsome. Does he have a good sense of humor?"

"Does any man?" she quipped.

"Come on, Kika. Is he funny or isn't he?"

She thought for a moment before replying, "Let's just say he's prone to unexpected bursts of humor."

"Interesting. So when are you going to see him again?"

"I'm having dinner with him this evening."

"Sounds like a date to me."

"It's business." Kika didn't want to confess that she had been thinking about doing more than dating Nick Miller. If Frannie knew the kind of fantasies Nick's kisses had generated, her matchmaking mind would be off to the races.

Actually, if Frannie knew that Nick had kissed her, she would never let the subject die. Besides, Kika didn't want her to know about the kisses. They were something she needed to understand herself before she told anyone else.

"I came to Tyler to get Fancy's Baby, not date the father of a prospective client." Kika tried to convince herself as well as her sister-in-law.

"So what's wrong with doing both?"

"Haven't you heard a word I said? First of all, it's a bad idea to mix business with pleasure. I want his daughter for a commercial, which automatically puts him out of the eligible field."

"Kika, I can name at least three men you've dated whom you met through work."

"And none of them worked out."

"I'm not suggesting you marry the guy." Frannie proceeded to lecture her as to the reasons why she should make the most of an opportunity to enjoy the company of a man like Nick Miller. Kika nodded her head as she listened, agreeing with her on most points. After all, they were things she had said to herself last night.

Nick was good-looking, he was obviously attracted to her, as she was to him, so what harm could come from spending some time with him? It would be a short-term thing, a matter of enjoying each other's company while the opportunity presented itself.

"Look at it this way, Kika. You might be able to convince the guy to let his daughter audition to be Fancy's Baby," Frannie added.

"I doubt it. He's dead set against it. It's more than likely I'll have to give up on the idea."

"I can't believe you said that! You, who are able to convince anyone to do anything?"

"This is different." Kika chuckled sardonically. "Frannie, I followed him around the carnival yesterday. I played games, watched a parade, even went on a Ferris wheel."

"You rode a Ferris wheel for this guy?"

"No, for Melody."

"What's she like? Is she as temperamental as she looks in the video?"

Kika's voice softened. "She's sweet, but very shy."

"That shouldn't be a problem. You have a talent for getting people to open up."

"Adult people."

"Are you worried she won't test well for Fancy's Baby?"

"Oh, I think she'll be perfect, but..." She paused, not wanting to admit that the problem was not with the little girl's suitability for the commercial, but with Kika herself. Her emotions were getting tied up with this assignment—something she had vowed would never happen. "I wish this job were over. You know I'm not very good with kids," Kika said with a sigh.

"That's not true," Frannie declared. "You just haven't had very many opportunities to be around them."

"You may be right. Look, I've got to go," she told her, not wanting to pursue the subject any further. "We'll talk when I get back next week."

Long after the phone call had ended, Kika lay in the hammock, thinking about her conversation with Frannie. Her sister-in-law was right about one thing—she hadn't had much experience with children.

Ever since she had lost Caroline, Kika had avoided being around kids, especially babies. Losing her daughter had left a wound that had refused to heal. No matter how hard she tried, she couldn't let go of the fear that she was incompetent as a mother. To the outside world she acted as if she had no interest in being one, when the truth of the matter was she was afraid to even think about the possibility.

But Frannie didn't know that. No one knew but her aunt Lucy, who had been at Kika's side when she had given birth to Caroline. Lucy had been her sole source of comfort when the doctor had saved Kika's life, an action that had resulted in the death of her infant daughter and had ended the possibility of her ever having any more children.

It had all happened in California, so neither her parents nor her brothers had any idea that she had even conceived a child. Only Aunt Lucy had known. She had nursed Kika back to health, consoled her through her grief and helped her put her life back together when there was no one else Kika could turn to for help.

Now, two years later, the pain was still there. Lucy had suggested she tell her parents about the baby, but Kika couldn't do it. Knowing she had had a child out of wedlock would break their hearts.

Besides, it was all in the past, although Kika's subconscious didn't seem to think so. No good could come out of telling her family now. It was just something she would have to live with. And she would. If it weren't for the fact that she was in the middle of the search for Fancy's Baby, she wouldn't even be thinking about it now.

She would get through this job, just as she had survived all the others that had involved kids. One thing she would have to do was ignore her attraction to Nick Miller. She couldn't afford to become emotionally involved with any man in Tyler. The object was to land a contract with Melody Miller, not let Nick Miller land her.

"DAD, YOU'RE NOT listening."

Guilt washed over Nick as he looked at his son. "Sorry. What did you say, Zach?"

"I said can we work on the go-cart?"

"Maybe after lunch."

"Dad!" Exasperation filled his voice.

"What?"

"You said maybe after breakfast. Now it's maybe after lunch. Next it'll be maybe after dinner." He shoved his fists to his chin, his elbows on the table.

"Well, this time I mean it. I have to finish reading this booklet. It's about the company I'm going to work for," Nick told his son, holding up the handbook for new employees.

Zachary leaned closer and said, "You've been on the same page all morning."

Nick knew it was true. He couldn't remember a thing he had read. That was because his mind was not on mechanical engineering, but on a shapely blonde who last night had made his whole body feel as if it were a Roman candle exploding into millions of sparkles.

"If we can't work on the go-cart, can we go swimming?" Zachary was already off on another subject.

Nick wasn't. Images of Kika Mancini danced in his head, taunting him. She thought she had the upper hand in their relationship. Relationship? A couple of kisses hardly constituted a relationship. It better not. He didn't want one. And if Ms. Kika Mancini thought he did, he was going to have to set her straight.

"Dad, you're not listening to me again," Zachary declared, interrupting his thoughts.

Nick looked at his son and realized he hadn't heard a word the boy had said. He set the handbook aside.

"We can work on the go-cart and go swimming this afternoon. But first I need to take care of some business," he told his son as he reached for the phone. "I'm going to get Abby to baby-sit for an hour or so and then we'll have the rest of the day together, okay?"

A half hour later Nick was in his convertible, top down, the wind blowing in his face as he drove the short distance to Timberlake Lodge. A pair of aviator sunglasses shaded his eyes from the bright summer sun. He was a man with a purpose.

When he arrived at the lodge, he realized that he should have called to see if Kika was even there. A visit to the front desk told him she wasn't in her room, but he knew she had to be somewhere in the vicinity because her rental car was parked outside. The clerk at the desk suggested he try the beach.

Following his directions, Nick took the footpath across the heavily wooded grounds to the swimming area. When he stepped onto the beach, there was no one in sight. There was, however, a red-and-white-striped towel on the sand. A pair of sandals, a denim shirt and a mystery novel occupied one end.

Automatically Nick's eyes went to the lake. Cutting gracefully through the clear blue water was a solitary figure. It was a woman. When she saw Nick watching, she swam toward the shore.

The sight of Kika Mancini emerging from the water in a lime-green bikini that barely covered the essential parts of her body was enough to make him forget the purpose of his visit. She squeezed the water from her hair as she walked toward him, obviously not the least bit uncomfortable with seeing him. Nick wished he could feel as relaxed as she looked.

"Hi." She gave him a dazzling smile that would have jump-started any normal man's hormone production. Nick was not a normal man. He hadn't been with a woman in nearly two years. The smile sent his hormones into overdrive.

"How's the water?" he asked, trying not to focus on her chest, where tiny droplets disappeared beneath the lime-green fabric. The thought of what lay beneath the scrap of material made the droplets magnets for his eyes.

"Cold at first, but once you're in, it's wonderfully refreshing." She picked up her towel and began patting the moisture from her skin.

His eyes traced her movements, watching as she dried her perfectly shaped arms, her slender thighs, her flat stomach. He noticed she had a tiny scar near her abdomen, a scar that was only visible when she lifted her arms over her head to drape the towel around her shoulders. As she covered herself, he felt both cheated and relieved.

"I'm surprised there aren't more people swimming," he commented, trying to act cool. At least his mirrored sunglasses hid his eyes.

She shrugged. "It's lunchtime, I guess. Too bad you didn't call before you came. I could have told you to bring your suit."

Was she flirting with him? If she was, she wouldn't be for long. He reminded himself of why he had come. He had a purpose.

"I think we need to get something straight," he began.

She had bent over to slip on her sandals. As she did, the view of her softly rounded backside with the lime-green bikini bottom riding up over a delectable round of flesh caused Nick to lose his concentration. He didn't continue.

She straightened and asked, "What is it?"

This was not going to be easy. "It's about last night."

"Is this going to take a while? Because if it is, maybe you'd like to get out of the sun."

Did he have sweat forming on his forehead or something? If there was one thing he hated it was being caught off guard, and she had a way of doing that to him when he least expected it.

"What I have to say will only take a few minutes," he told her a bit more sharply than he intended.

She shrugged and, to his surprise, gave him a grin, spreading her arms as she said, "The sand's all yours."

Nick knew that if he was going to sound intelligent, he was going to have to look at the lake, not at her. He focused on a sailboat that was drifting with the gentle breeze.

"When I'm with you I find myself doing things I normally wouldn't do," he told her.

"I'm going to take that as a compliment. From what I can see, your world is much too dull, Nick Miller."

Out of the corner of his eye he noticed she was moving. He glanced at her to discover she had dropped the towel from her shoulders and tied it around her waist, leaving her torso bare except for the lime-green strings attached to skimpy triangles of cloth.

"Dull or not, it's my world, Kika. That's why that kiss last night—"

"You mean kisses, don't you, Nick?" she interrupted.

"All right, those kisses," he conceded. "Those kisses meant nothing."

"Nothing?" She arched one eyebrow.

"Nothing."

"I see."

"Good." He would have said more, but his gaze was trapped by the shapely flesh bulging forth from the lime-green triangles. Blood rushed to every corner of his body and especially to a place where he didn't want it to be. Those kisses meant nothing, he repeated silently. "You're a casting director in Minneapolis and I'm a mechanical engineer in Tyler," he reminded her.

"Which means?"

"After the auditions are completed, you'll go your way and I'll go mine."

"You're not telling me anything I don't already know, Nick."

He wished she wouldn't say his name. She had a way of making it sound like a term of endearment.

"Then we understand each other, right?" he asked.

"Definitely. I'm here on business. We both know that." She stared at the sand and started drawing circles with her toe.

"Then it's probably better if we don't have dinner together tonight," he stated quietly.

That brought her head up with a jerk. He could see she was disappointed. "You're not going to give me one more chance to convince you Melody would be a good candidate for Fancy's Baby?"

"I thought you said dinner was a thank-you for getting your car unlocked."

"It is, but I am here on business," she reminded him with a cheeky grin that begged for forgiveness. "Come on, Nick. Say yes."

Despite his earlier resolution, Nick didn't want to say no. It had been a long time since he had been out with a woman. Cece had suggested he think about dating again, and even Annabelle was trying to set him up with someone. Though, tonight would be a business dinner, it would give him a chance to ease back into the social scene.

"You said seven, right?" he asked.

Satisfaction gleamed in Kika's eyes. "Seven," she echoed. "Here at the lodge, casual-like."

He nodded, then averted his eyes as she bent to pick up the rest of her things.

He must have frowned, for she said, "You don't need to worry, Nick. The record is straight."

"Good."

When he turned to leave, she said, "I'm glad you stopped by."

"So am I."

As he drove home he tried to rationalize what had happened. He couldn't. Nor did he want to. All he could think about was how her body had looked in that bikini.

CHAPTER EIGHT

"HOW COME we can't go with you?" Patrick demanded as his father headed for the shower.

"Because you're having dinner at Auntie Cece's," Nick answered, then closed the bathroom door with decisive force.

Thank heaven for Auntie Cece, Nick silently prayed as the warm water pelted his skin. When sixteen-year-old Abby had turned down his offer of a baby-sitting job, he had seen it as a sign he shouldn't be having dinner with Kika. But then Cece had phoned to invite the kids over for pizza. If opportunity knocked, he'd be foolish to ignore it, right?

When he had finished showering and shaving, he found Patrick still hanging around waiting for him. "Why can't you bring Kika over to Auntie Cece's?" the six-year-old asked as he followed Nick into his bedroom.

"I'm not sure she likes pizza," Nick answered, opening his closet doors and assessing his wardrobe with a critical eye. Everything looked old and worn, reminding him that he hadn't paid much attention to his clothes since Beth had died.

He remembered Annabelle had given him a new shirt for his birthday. It was buried somewhere in the stack of cartons still waiting to be unpacked. After a brief search, he found it in its original box.

"Is that a new shirt, Dad?"

"Yeah. What do you think?" Nick held it to his chest for his son's inspection.

"It's nice. I like green."

Nick didn't, which was why he hadn't worn it yet. He would have returned it, but he hadn't wanted to offend Annabelle. Now, as he surveyed it, he was glad he had kept it. At least it was new and wrinkle free.

He pulled it on and stood in front of the mirror. It made his stomach look flat, his arms muscular. Maybe Annabelle knew more about fashion that he had given her credit for.

Coupled with the khaki trousers he had just picked up from the launderers, the shirt looked surprisingly good. Kika had said casual. He gave himself one last look in the mirror, then grabbed his keys from the dresser and headed down the stairs, Patrick trailing behind.

As he passed the family room, he paused, calling out to Zachary, "It's time to go to Auntie Cece's. Did you pack a bag for Melody?"

"It's next to the front door," Zachary answered as he turned off the TV.

"Great." Nick glanced at his watch. "Where's your sister?"

"She's hiding behind the sofa. I don't think she wants to go," Zachary answered.

Nick walked around the brown plaid sectional and found his daughter huddled in the corner, her arms wrapped around the white teddy bear Kika had given her. Nick crouched beside her and held out his hand.

"Come on, Mel," he coaxed. "It's time to go."

She didn't move a muscle, but sat staring at him, her tiny cheeks a rosy pink.

"You don't want to go over to Auntie Cece's?"

The red head slowly moved from side to side.

"You can bring your bear."

Patrick had climbed up onto the couch and was perched over the back, his arms dangling close to where Nick squatted. "Maybe she wants a peanut butter samwich."

Nick thought it was worth a shot. "Would you like me to make you a peanut butter sandwich to take along?"

Again, she shook her head.

"I think she wants to go with you, Dad," Zachary informed him from the opposite end of the sofa.

Something in the way that angelic little face looked at him made Nick disregard the inner voice that begged him to ignore the possibility and ask, "Would you like to have dinner with me and Kika?"

Melody nodded.

Nick's stomach tightened. What he didn't need was to take a toddler on a date. Yet he was certain that if he forced Melody to stay at her cousin's, she'd have one of her temper tantrums. How could he leave a screaming, kicking toddler with his sister-in-law?

It was a battle between common sense and hormones. Maybe he should bring his daughter along. That way he wouldn't get any ideas that this dinner was anything more than a casting agent's attempt to get him to agree to an audition.

Nick stood, shoving his hands to his hips. "All right. Melody will come with me."

"No fair!" A duet of complaints filled the air.

"How come she can go but we can't?" Patrick asked.

"Dad, you always let her get her way," Zachary protested.

Nick was in no mood to defend his actions to his sons. "She's coming with me and you two are going to Auntie Cece's. That's all that's going to be said." He held out his hand to Melody, who willingly placed her tiny one into it.

While the boys grumbled and stamped their way to the car, she walked smugly beside her father, dragging the big white bear behind her. Nick knew what they said was true. Melody did usually get her way. It wasn't what he wanted, but under the circumstances, what choice did he have?

Fortunately, by the time they arrived at Cece's and the boys saw that Jeff had put up a tent for them to use as a fort, all thoughts of spending the evening with Nick and Kika disappeared. Melody, however, was not so easily distracted.

"There's been a change in plans," Nick announced to his brother-in-law as the boys made a beeline for the tent. "Melody wants to go with me."

"Is that going to work for you?" Jeff asked as Nick propped himself against the right fender of the Mustang.

He shrugged. "It'll be okay."

Jeff leaned over the door of the convertible and spoke to Melody. "Don't you want to come inside and see Annie and Belle?"

The toddler shook her head. The look Jeff cast in Nick's direction was full of sympathy. "I bet Cece would give you some ice cream." Jeff dangled the temptation shamelessly.

Still Melody showed no interest, prompting Nick to say in a tone audible only to Jeff, "I've tried the bribery thing and it doesn't work."

"What are you going to do with your date? Make her sit in the back seat?" Jeff looked pointedly at the toddler's car seat strapped into the passenger side of the Mustang.

"It's not a date," Nick contradicted, although he knew it was simply a question of semantics. "It's a business meeting. How do you know about it, anyway?"

"Cece ran into Kika this afternoon."

"So that's why the pizza party happened."

Jeff grinned. "We figured you could use a little help."

"Yes, well, I appreciate it, but this isn't exactly working out as I had planned," Nick admitted, rubbing a hand across his smooth jaw.

"Why don't you come inside for a cold drink and we'll see what we can do? Annie and Belle are playing inside," he said with a wink.

Nick knew what the other man was up to. He hoped that once Melody saw her cousins, she would want to stay and play.

It didn't happen. Melody clung to Nick as he sat at the kitchen table, refusing to even get down from his lap. Although she looked with interest at Annie and Belle playing with their doll buggies, she didn't want to join them.

Finally, Cece took matters into her own hands, cajoling and coaxing the toddler with a gentleness that reminded Nick of Beth. After only a few minutes, she was able to get Melody to sit on her lap.

It wasn't long before Melody was on the floor playing with her cousins. When Nick announced it was time he get going, Cece suggested he leave Melody behind with the boys.

"I can't do that. She'd be screaming before I got out the door," Nick said in a low voice.

"She wouldn't be the first child to cry when her parent leaves," Cece assured him. "Nick, it's common for kids her age to put up a fuss when Mom or Dad wants to go away."

Nick sighed. "Melody's different. You must have noticed that by now." It wasn't an easy admission.

Cece put a hand on his shoulder. "She's missed out on something most little girls have, that's true, but that's why you brought her here. She needs to be with other kids, to be with family who love her and want to be there for her. Let us be tonight, okay?"

He knew what she said was true, but still he hesitated.

"Trust me on this one, Nick," she persuaded gently.

"All right, but I hope you realize what you're letting yourself in for. She can throw quite a temper tantrum," he warned.

"She'll be fine," Cece said confidently.

As much as Nick wanted to believe that, he had his doubts as he walked away. Before he could get out the door, Melody caught him by the leg, tugging on his trousers.

As he drove away from Cece's, his heart ached. He wanted to rush back in and take her with him, yet the things Cece had said made sense. Melody did need to be with other kids and she did need a woman's influence. If only she hadn't looked at him as if he was the most important person in her life and he was abandoning her.

Several times on the way to Timberlake Lodge Nick was tempted to turn around and go back to Cece's. Only one thing kept him going straight: hormones.

KIKA BUTTONED UP the bodice of the pink knit dress and said, "Man the torpedoes and full speed ahead." She eyed herself critically in the full-length mirror and was satisfied with the results.

She almost hadn't packed the dress Frannie called her "manhunter," a sleeveless ribbed knit with a split skirt. "Fit with flare," was how the salesclerk had described it.

It clung in all the right places but flowed freely about Kika's legs. She had thrown it in at the last minute just in case she needed it. It would be interesting to see Nick Miller's reaction to it.

Ever since he had told her their kisses had meant nothing, her ego had needed a little nurturing. Not that she believed for one minute that he wasn't just as attracted to her as she was to him. He was. Having worked for seven years in the entertainment industry, she could recognize desire in a man's eyes when she saw it.

There was a chemistry between them, pure and simple. Kika had felt it that first night she saw him in the airport. She didn't like the fact any more than he did. All she could hope was that it would run its course and not interfere with the work she was here to do.

At six fifty-five he rang her room to let her know he would meet her on the verandah. Kika slipped on a pair of sandals, grabbed her wallet-on-a-string and headed for the main entrance.

She found him gazing up at the antique canoe hanging from the rafters. When he saw her, he lost the carefree look that had been on his face only seconds before. Instead of being invited to dinner, he could have been waiting in line to donate blood.

She stepped up to him. "Hi."

As she had expected, the dress caught his attention. Nick Miller could tell himself all night long that the kisses between them had meant nothing, but there was no way he was going to convince her that he wasn't attracted to her. It was there in his eyes.

As if he didn't want her to see that attraction, he looked up at the old canoe once more. "This is an interesting place."

"Isn't it though? It's an old hunting lodge. Can't you just sense the presence of men smoking pipes and carrying their rifles?" Kika remarked. "Come. I'll show you the dining room." She slipped her arm through his and led him down a hallway.

He wore that same scent Kika had noticed the first time she had met him. As before, it teased her senses and made her want to get closer to him.

She had prepaid for dinner so no check would be brought and had made sure they would have a private table in the dining room. As the waitress handed them menus, Nick smiled, and Kika saw his dimples crease his cheeks. Her heart fluttered.

As soon as the specials of the evening had been rattled off and their beverage orders had been taken, the waitress disappeared. So did Nick's smile. Kika wanted it to return.

"Well, what do you think?" she asked. "Are you going to try the beer cheese soup?"

"Have you had it before?"

"Sure. They serve it in Minnesota. It's pretty good." She leaned closer to him and whispered, "Wisconsin sports fans are known as cheeseheads."

He grinned. "I know. I watch football and I've seen the hats."

He turned his attention back to the menu. Kika waited for him to say something—anything—but he didn't. Finally, he closed the menu and set it aside.

"This is an interesting place," he remarked, taking an inventory of the wood-panelled room.

"You said that already," she reminded him. He didn't look the least embarrassed. "What else do you find interesting, Nick?" she asked provocatively.

"Your dress," he answered, glancing at the low-cut bodice.

"My sister-in-law calls it a manhunter."

"Is that a warning?"

"You don't strike me as the kind of man who needs to be forewarned," she answered, her bruised ego searching for a balm.

"Depends on the danger." He held her gaze and her heartbeat increased its pace.

"I've never been called dangerous—at least, not to my face."

"Probably because a lot of men like to flirt with trouble." It looked as if the dimples would reappear, but he held them in check.

"You think I'm trouble, Nick?"

His eyes dropped to her bodice and a grin slowly revealed his teeth and the dimples. "In that dress you might be."

The waitress returned with their drinks, temporarily preempting their sexual banter. As soon as she was gone, Kika said, "I have to confess. All afternoon I expected you to call and tell me you weren't going to come tonight."

"Now why would I want to do that?"

"You haven't been exactly *eager* to discuss business with me," she reminded him.

"You know I don't like the idea of my daughter being in commercials," he said honestly.

"She doesn't have to make a career out of it. Just this one-shot deal would probably make her enough money to fund her college education." Once again Kika was the persuasive talent agent.

"I don't think you're going to change my mind," he warned her.

"There are still a few days before the auditions begin." She lifted her wineglass in salute. "In the meantime, thank you—for getting the keys out of my locked car."

"You're welcome." He smiled and her stomach fluttered.

"So tell me. Did you grow up on the West Coast or was it your work that took you there?" She clasped her hands in her lap so he wouldn't see her fidgeting.

"I was born and raised in L.A."

"And did you like growing up in sunny California?"

He shrugged. "It was a lot different when I was a kid. Fewer people, fewer cars, less pollution. I didn't mind leaving."

"So you don't miss it?"

"Not so far, but then it's still summer. I suppose once the snow falls I'll miss the sunshine and mild temperatures."

"Does the rest of your family still live there?"

He shook his head. "They're scattered across the country. My parents retired to Arizona, I have one brother in Seattle and one in Philadelphia."

"I can't imagine what it would be like to have my family so far apart. I have three brothers and we all live within five miles of each other."

"You're lucky your profession hasn't demanded that you move away," he commented.

"I did live in L.A. for a couple of years."

"And what did you think of it?"

It was a painful period of her life that she really didn't want to discuss. "It was all right, but I prefer the Midwest. I like being near my family."

"Then you're close to your brothers?"

"If you're Italian, you're close to brothers, sisters, aunts, uncles, great-aunts, great-uncles...." She trailed off with an affectionate grin. "Actually, my brothers are terrific. It's just that they think they need to protect me."

"If you wear that dress very often I can understand why." His eyes lingered just a little too long on the bodice, and her body grew warm.

"I don't need a man to fight my battles," she stated defiantly. "I can take care of myself."

He cracked a half smile. "I believe you can."

"To survive in the entertainment industry, a woman has to be tough," she assured him.

"And you find it's worth the struggle?"

"Most of the time." She didn't want to admit to him that there had been times when the headaches of the job overshadowed the rewards.

That topic came to an end as the waitress returned to take their orders. When she had finished, an awkward silence stretched between Kika and Nick. It was broken by a young boy who approached their table carrying a basket of roses.

"Would you like to support the Little League of Tyler?" He stopped beside Nick, giving him a chance to appraise the flowers.

Nick reached in his pocket for his wallet and pulled out a few bills. Although there were several red roses in the basket, he selected a pale pink flower nestled in a sprig of baby's breath and offered it to Kika.

"Thank you." She sniffed it appreciatively. "Pink is my favorite color. Plus it matches my dress." She held the flower across her chest and Nick thought she had never looked lovelier.

As they dined by candlelight, he realized that he was falling a little in love with the energetic blonde. The more she told him about herself, the more he wanted to know. Hating to have the evening end, he suggested they go for a walk when they had finished eating.

She readily agreed and led him down to the lake, where the setting sun cast a peachy glow on the water. Tied to the wooden dock was a white fiberglass canoe.

"Oh, good. No one's using it." Kika walked over to the canoe and squatted down. "Do you know how to paddle one of these things?"

"I haven't done it before," he admitted, watching her carefully climb aboard.

"It's easy, especially when the water is this calm." She held on to the dock and motioned for him to get in. "Come on. I'll show you."

Nick hesitated for only a minute, then stepped into the narrow boat behind her, careful not to upset the tippy craft. As soon as he was seated, Kika untied the rope securing the canoe to the dock.

"We need to work together to move smoothly," she told him as she reached for a paddle. He followed her lead, dipping the other paddle in the water in time with her strokes.

"You must have done this before," he observed as they maneuvered the boat across the placid lake.

"Lots of times. When we were kids my folks often took us up to the Boundary Waters in northern Minnesota, where we'd spend a week canoeing," she told him.

Within a few minutes, they were far out from shore. A multitude of colors shaded the western sky, and they were bathed in the amber glow of sunset.

"Well, what do you think?" Kika asked when they finally rested their paddles across the gunwales and floated for a moment.

Nick thought the view was spectacular, mainly because Kika was in the center of it. He knew there was no point denying it. She had aroused a part of him that had been sleeping for two years, and it felt good to be alive.

Out in the middle of the lake, gently bobbing in the canoe, they talked and laughed until all the color had faded from the sky.

"We should head back before it gets too dark and we can't see the shoreline," Kika told him.

Reluctantly, Nick dipped his paddle back into the water. When they coasted alongside the dock, he climbed out first and offered Kika a hand. She got out gracefully and secured the boat to the dock.

They stood like statues in the twilight, facing each other without saying a word. A loose tendril of hair had fallen across her cheek. Nick brushed it back with his fingers. As his flesh grazed hers, she trembled and looked up at him with an invitation in her eyes.

She wanted him to kiss her.

Slowly, he lowered his head and placed his lips over hers in a kiss that was as gentle as the waves that lapped against the side of the canoe.

It was like falling into the sunset, Nick decided, his body warm and glowing as they kissed. When his lips parted hers, she rubbed against him in a seductive manner, causing every nerve in his body to vibrate with desire.

One kiss became two, then three, then four. Hands that had clung to shoulders explored unfamiliar territory, creating sighs of pleasure. How far they would have gone was a question that went unanswered, for just then a trio of yodelers began to sing.

Whether they were close by or across the lake was impossible to tell in the still night air. Reluctantly, Nick released her, experiencing a sense of loss as she pulled back from him.

The moon was rising over the lake, casting a silvery sheen on the calm water. Still close to the horizon, it made a stunning statement against the indigo sky.

"I want to see you again, Kika," Nick heard himself say.

"I'd like that, too," she said softly.

"I'm taking the kids to Lake Michigan tomorrow. Would you like to come along?"

She hesitated before answering. "I have a couple of appointments during the day, but I could meet you for dinner."

His first thought was that she didn't want to be around his kids. He was about to tell her that he had plans for tomorrow evening when she said, "Wait. I'll reschedule the appointments. What time should I expect you?"

"Nine." And with one last quick kiss, he left.

ALL THE WAY back to Cece and Jeff's, Nick debated whether he should call Kika and tell her that tomorrow wasn't going to work out. But then he remembered how good her lips had felt and he knew he would do no such thing.

When he arrived he found Melody sitting on her aunt's lap, listening to her read a story. Nick expected his daughter to come running once she noticed him, but she didn't. She appeared to be perfectly content in Cece's arms.

Seeing them together made Nick realize how much Melody missed having a mother. Cece had the same gentle spirit as Beth, and the way she got Melody to respond was a sad reminder of what was missing in his daughter's life.

For the past two years he had been so caught up in his own grief that he hadn't fully realized the extent of Melody's loss. Here was a little girl who had never known the woman who had died giving her life. She hadn't had a mother to sing her lullabies at night or cook her breakfast in the morning. All she had was a father who didn't know the first thing about mother-daughter relationships. Melody had three males in her life. What she needed now was a mother, a feminine role model.

Immediately he thought of Kika. She was beautiful, she was vibrant, she was fun to be with. There was only one small problem: she wasn't maternal.

"Your daughter's a night owl," Cece said affectionately, interrupting his musings. "Beth always liked to stay up late, too."

Nick smiled reflectively. "Are you ready to go home, Mel?" He sat down beside the two of them.

Melody shook her head. "Where are the boys?" he asked, glancing around the room.

"Still in the tent. They took a couple of flashlights and a stack of Jeff's old comics and I haven't heard from them since." Cece gently eased Melody from her lap. "I'll call them."

As she headed toward the kitchen, Melody scrambled down from the sofa to tag behind her.

Nick reached for her canvas tote and began picking up her scattered toys.

"So how was your evening?" Cece asked when she returned.

"Great," Nick answered, unsure as to how much he should say about his evening with Kika.

"The lodge has good food, doesn't it?"

"Umm-hmm," he agreed. "We went canoeing on the lake after dinner. It was very scenic."

Cece eyed him curiously. "Kika's a nice person."

"Yes, she is."

He was relieved when the boys came barreling into the living room, for he didn't want to discuss his relationship with Kika. Zach and Patrick begged Nick to let them sleep over in the tent. After a discussion

with Cece, it was agreed that they could borrow the
tent so that they could sleep outside the following
night. Excited, they eagerly climbed into the car. To
Nick's relief, Melody didn't put up a fuss, either,
when he strapped her into her car seat.

Before Nick got behind the driver's wheel, Cece
asked, "Have you thought any more about letting
Melody audition for the Fancy's Baby ad?"

"I'm considering it," he said, surprising himself.
Turning his back so the kids wouldn't hear the conversation, he said, "The trouble is I've lived in California and I've seen what can happen to kids in show
business."

"You have to do what you think is best," Cece said
as a vote of confidence.

Nick knew she was right. On the way home he
thought about Beth. He wondered if she would have
approved of Melody auditioning for Fancy's Baby.

She was still on his mind when he went to bed that
night. However, when he finally fell asleep, it wasn't
Beth's face in his thoughts, but his daughter's. She
needed a mother, and so far the only woman he had
been attracted to was Kika, who had said she didn't
want to be around any more babies.

CHAPTER NINE

KIKA DIDN'T WANT to analyze what was happening between her and Nick. She had told herself that she was seeing him to try to convince him that Melody was right for Fancy's Baby, but she knew she was only fooling herself. Last night had been a date, not a business meeting, and the true reason she was seeing him again had little to do with his daughter.

When he arrived at the lodge the following morning, the top was up on his convertible. Melody's car seat was in the center of the back seat, nestled between the two boys. All three kids smiled when they saw her, warming her heart.

Dressed in a faded pair of jeans and a cream-colored T-shirt, Nick looked even more attractive to Kika than he had the night before. When she would have climbed in on the passenger side of the Mustang, he suggested she might like to drive. Delighted, she eagerly slid behind the wheel and listened patiently as Nick explained the instrument panel.

"This is great!" she exclaimed as the little red car ate up the miles on the highway. "I like it."

"We need to take the next exit," Nick told her, looking up from the map on his lap.

He guided her to a marina, where row after row of sailboats lined the narrow piers. When he had said they would be going to Lake Michigan, she had expected they would swim and sun on the beach. Nick, however, had other ideas. After a quick stop at a deli, they rented a sailboat and spent the afternoon on the water.

She discovered that although he had little experience with canoe paddles, he was a seasoned sailor. Kika could hardly believe she had ever accused the man of not knowing how to have fun. By the end of the afternoon they were sunburned and windblown, but Kika couldn't remember the last time she had enjoyed herself more.

When she returned to the lodge, there were several messages waiting. One was from Glenna McRoberts, who had left her home number. "I have good news for you," Glenna told her when she returned her call. "Melody Miller's name is on the audition roster."

Stunned, Kika asked, "When did that happen?"

"This morning. I thought maybe you already knew about it."

Kika wondered if Glenna knew she and Nick had been out together. "No, I didn't know, but I'm delighted."

"There are more than two hundred names."

"That's great!" Kika said enthusiastically. She made arrangements to stop by TylerTots the following morning.

As she showered and blow-dried her hair, Kika wondered what it was that had made Nick change his mind about letting Melody try out for the part. And why he hadn't mentioned it when they were together.

Wanting to talk to him, she drove into Tyler after dinner. As she pulled up in front of his house, she saw Zachary creeping behind the picket fence, a plastic bazooka in his hand. Following close on his heels was Patrick, carrying a toy machine gun.

Kika climbed out of the car and followed the sidewalk around to the backyard. She could see Melody sitting in the sandbox, a shovel in one hand, a fistful of dirt in the other. There was no sign of Nick anywhere.

Kika unlatched the wooden gate. It creaked as she slowly pushed it open. Before she had taken two steps into the yard, a deluge of water hit her in the face.

"Aha! I got you," Nick called in delight as he leapt out in front of her. The glee on his face changed to a look of horror when he realized his mistake.

Kika was too stunned to speak. Water ran in rivulets down her face, her hair was plastered to her skull and her clothes clung to her skin.

"Kika! I'm sorry!" he exclaimed, dropping the plastic bucket as if it were on fire.

The boys came barreling through the gate behind her, guns aimed at their father. When they saw what had happened, their mouths fell open.

"You got Kika!" Patrick exclaimed, eyes wide.

"Zachary, run inside and get a towel," Nick ordered, then led the drenched Kika over to the picnic table.

"We were having a water fight." Patrick announced the obvious.

"I'm really sorry, Kika. I thought you were one of the boys," Nick said penitently.

Kika looked down at her white T-shirt. Because it was wet, not only was her bra apparent, her nipples were as well. When she glanced at Nick, she saw that he had noticed, too.

Zachary came charging out of the house with a fluffy yellow towel. Nick took it from him and draped it around her shoulders.

"We weren't expecting company," he said a bit sheepishly. "When I heard the gate opening I thought the boys were trying to sneak up on me." When she still didn't say anything, he said, "I do believe this is the first time I've seen you at a loss for words."

"Better enjoy it. It won't last," she warned him, running her fingers through her damp curls.

"Do you want to be on our side?" Patrick asked, waving his finger back and forth between him and his brother. "I have two squirt guns."

As if he could read her thoughts, Nick said, "Do you want the boys to tie me up so you can use my face for target practice?"

"It's tempting," Kika answered, using the corner of the towel to dab at her wet cheeks.

"Are we going to play or not?" Zachary demanded, his super squirter on his hip.

"I think we're about done for this evening," Nick answered. "We need to take Kika inside so she can dry off."

Melody had climbed out of the sandbox and was standing off to one side, quietly observing the situation. When Kika caught her eye, the little girl smiled shyly. Kika felt as if someone had brushed a feather across her skin.

"Pick up after Mel, guys," Nick instructed his sons. He scooped the toddler up in his arms and started toward the house, gesturing for Kika to follow.

As soon as Kika stepped inside the house, she could tell no woman lived there. There was a box of cereal on the kitchen table, a pile of newspapers in the corner, and the countertops were littered with dishes. If there was one thing Nick Miller wasn't, it was neat.

He didn't seem the least bit put out that she had caught him in a mess. He set Melody down, then led Kika along a hallway to the bathroom, which was surprisingly orderly. He opened a vanity drawer and pulled out a hair dryer.

"You can use this."

"Thanks."

"Do you think you should dry your clothes?" he asked, his eyes lingering briefly on her still-transparent top. "I have a shirt you could put on."

"That's probably a good idea," she answered. They didn't need any added stimulation; there was already enough sexual tension between them.

He disappeared only to return a few moments later with a denim shirt dangling from his finger. She took it from him and closed the bathroom door. As she peeled off her T-shirt, she realized her bra was also wet. Should she give him that to dry as well? After a short deliberation, she stripped off the satin undergarment and slipped on the denim shirt, buttoning all but the top button.

"If you show me where the dryer is, I'll take care of this," she told Nick when she opened the door again.

"I'll do it," he insisted, reaching for the wet T-shirt.

Not wanting him to see the bra inside, Kika held the T-shirt in a ball in her fist. "No, I'll do it."

"Don't be silly," he said, prying it from her hands.

They did a little tug of war until finally the satin bra tumbled out of the folded shirt, landing on the floor.

Kika felt her face grow warm as she stooped to pick up the undergarment.

"I've been married, Kika. I know what they look like," he told her with a gleam in his eye.

She handed him the T-shirt and bra. "Put it on a low setting, please."

"Will do," he said, then disappeared down the hallway. When she went to close the bathroom door again, Melody stood in the way.

"Want to come inside?" Kika asked, expecting the toddler to turn and run. She didn't. Shyly, she crept across the bathroom floor. She pulled a wooden stool from the corner and shoved it next to the vanity. Then she climbed up on the stool and leaned her chubby little arms on the counter.

Kika shut the door and was about to plug in the dryer when she noticed Melody eyeing her partially open purse. Curiosity was written all over her face.

"Would you like to look inside?" Kika asked.

Tiny fingers covered with dirt were about to reach for the leather bag when Kika said, "How about if we wash our hands first?" Melody was silent. "Come. I'll lift you and we can do it together."

Again, she didn't expect the toddler to do as she suggested, but to her surprise, Melody went into her outstretched arms. She was warm and soft and smelled like baby powder. Kika felt a rush of conflicting emotions. She wanted to hold this precious little girl, yet she felt awkward at the same time.

She twisted the faucet handles, sending a stream of water cascading over two large and two small hands. When she would have squirted a dab of liquid soap on Melody's hands, the toddler protested. Kika soon discovered the reason why. Melody wanted to get her own soap. She could push down the pump handle on the dispenser and took great pleasure in doing so.

When hands had been soaped, rinsed and dried, Kika set Melody on the vanity top with her purse in front of her. Then she plugged in the hair dryer.

With a practiced ease, she used her fingers to fluff up her hair as she moved the dryer over her blond tresses. Melody watched, the purse no longer the object of her attention. Occasionally, Kika would aim the hot air at the toddler, who would giggle at the sensation.

A pounding on the door had Kika shutting off the dryer and twisting the knob. Nick stood in the hallway.

"Is Melody in there?"

"Umm-hmm. She's right here." She opened the door completely so that he could see his daughter.

"Come on, Mel. We need to leave Kika alone," Nick said, reaching for her.

But she didn't want to leave. She snatched her hand away from his and shook her head, grunting in what Kika had come to recognize as a "no."

"It's all right. She can stay," Kika told him. "I'm almost done."

Without a hairbrush to tame her blond tresses, Kika knew she resembled a wild woman. And from the way Nick was looking at her, he must have thought the same thing.

"I'll wait in the other room."

Kika nodded, then finished with the hair dryer. When she was done, she applied a light dusting of powder on her cheeks and a thin covering of gloss on her lips. Seeing Melody's fascination with the process, she took her makeup brush and gently stroked the tiny cheeks. Melody giggled.

When Kika was finished, she took Melody by the hand and went to look for Nick. She found him in the kitchen, shoving toys into a closet. When he saw her, his eyes darkened appreciatively.

"Would you like something to drink while you wait?" he asked. "We've got lemonade, fruit juice, soda...."

"Lemonade would be nice," she answered, sitting down on the chrome-and-vinyl chair.

"What about you, Mel? Do you want some lemonade?" Nick asked his daughter.

She nodded, then, to Kika's surprise, held out her arms, indicating she wanted to be lifted onto her lap. Nick's face mirrored Kika's own shock.

"Here, Mel. You have your own chair." He was about to reach for her, but Kika stopped him.

"It's okay. She can sit with me." She was rewarded with a smile from the toddler. Again, conflicting emotions tore at Kika's heart. She wanted to cherish this little girl. The intensity of her feelings frightened her. She knew it was foolish to think that she could be a mother to any child.

Nick looked as uneasy as she felt. He took a red plastic pitcher from the refrigerator and set it on the table. "I'll get you a glass," he said a bit gruffly.

"What about Melody?"

He went to the cupboard and pulled out a cup with two handles. He poured a small amount of lemonade into it. Melody gulped it down, then held up her empty cup for Kika to refill.

Nick continued to clean the kitchen, occasionally looking at the two of them seated at the table. Finally, Kika broke the silence. "Nick, if you don't want me here, just say so."

He stopped putting things away and stared at her for several moments. Then he came over to the table and took the chair beside her, laying his arm across the back of hers, his other arm on the table.

"I do want you here. I love the way you look seated at my kitchen table wearing my shirt." His voice had a huskiness to it that made Kika want to reach out and touch him.

She didn't need to, because he touched her first. He took her hand and brought it to his lips. Kika's insides threatened to dissolve. She had to look away from his penetrating gaze or risk doing something she knew she shouldn't do.

"Do you know what it does to me to see you sitting here in my shirt when I know that you have nothing on underneath?"

Kika's whole body grew warm. He hadn't released her hand and she could feel his other one on her shoulder. Had he been kissing her the moment couldn't have been more erotic.

Just when she thought he was going to, he asked, "Why did you come over tonight?"

Kika realized now that it hadn't been to thank him for letting his daughter audition; that had just been an excuse. What she really wanted was to be with him. To be in his arms. To feel his lips on hers.

Before she could answer, however, there was a knock on the back door. It was Annabelle.

"I brought you some homemade jam," she said as she stepped into the entry way. Because the table and chairs were in an alcove of the kitchen, she didn't immediately notice Kika.

When she did, her smile disappeared. Actually, her mouth dropped open in horror.

Kika could see that the woman had obviously misread the situation. Not that she blamed her. With Nick's oversize denim shirt hiding her shorts, it looked as if she was wearing nothing else. And then there was her hair. The way it stood on end, anyone might have thought she had been romping around on a bed.

Obviously, that was exactly what Annabelle thought. "Oh! You're not alone."

"No, Kika's here," Nick confirmed.

There were several more moments of awkward silence, then Annabelle said, "Should I make some tea?"

"I'm not sure I have any," Nick answered.

"Yes, you do. I left some the other day," Annabelle told him, moving over to the cupboard. "I bet there's a teakettle somewhere in here. Every house has one."

Not mine, Kika wanted to declare boldly, but she decided to hold her tongue. Feeling the need to justify her presence, she explained, "I stopped by to thank Nick for signing Melody up for the audition."

Annabelle slammed the tea kettle down on the burner. "What did you say?"

Too late Kika realized that Nick hadn't told his mother-in-law the news. She could see she had made a mistake by the look on Annabelle's face.

"I thought we agreed that wasn't a good idea." Annabelle looked to her son-in-law for an explanation.

"I think Melody will do just fine," he said reassuringly.

Annabelle stood speechless, staring at him with a look of betrayal on her face. However, she didn't lose her voice for long. "How can you do this to her? Melody's not like other children. She's special. Do you really want her to be under those bright lights and have a camera following her around?"

"It's only one commercial," Nick said patiently.

Annabelle harrumphed. "It's show business," she said with distaste. "I can't believe you're going to do this. What did this woman do to make you change your mind?"

It was at that point that Kika felt it was best to leave the room. "If you'll excuse me, I think I'll check on my clothes." She set Melody down on the floor as she stood.

"Come sit on Grandma's lap," Annabelle said as Kika started to walk away.

Melody, however, had other ideas. She ran after Kika, tugging on the tail of the denim shirt. Kika gave Nick a helpless look.

He looked as though he wanted to grab Melody himself, but to her surprise he said, "It's okay. She can go with you, if you don't mind." There was a plea for understanding in his eyes.

"No, it's all right," she answered, taking the little girl by the hand. As she left she could hear Annabelle saying, "Do you think it's wise to have a woman sitting in your kitchen with nothing on but a shirt—your shirt—when you have young children in this house?"

Kika didn't hear Nick's answer. She made herself scarce in the laundry room for several minutes, talking to Melody. When the dryer finally stopped Kika put her clothes back on, then went back to face the dragon—which was how she was coming to view Annabelle.

When she entered the kitchen, however, the postmistress was gone. Nick was scooping out chocolate ice cream for Patrick and Zachary, who sat at the table.

"You want some ice cream, Kika?" Patrick asked when she entered the room.

"No, but I bet Melody does," Kika answered.

The toddler ran to her high chair and held her arms out to Kika.

"She wants you to put her in her chair," Patrick explained. "I'll get her spoon." He walked over to a drawer while Kika settled Melody in her chair. Feeling a bit awkward standing around doing nothing, Kika asked Nick, "Can I help?"

"I'm fine," he answered rather abruptly.

It didn't take a genius to figure out that he was angry. The question was, with her or with Annabelle? As much as Kika wanted it to be his mother-in-law, she had the uneasy feeling that she had brought the scowl to his face.

In silence, he gave each of his children a dish of ice cream. The only chatter came from the boys, who were still talking about the water fight.

When Nick made no attempt to speak to her, but turned his attention to loading glasses into the dishwasher, Kika said, "I should probably get going."

She waited for him to say something. When he didn't, she knew it was best to leave. She picked up her purse and headed toward the door.

"I'm sorry about mentioning Melody's audition like that," she apologized as she passed him. "I didn't know you hadn't told Annabelle."

"Didn't you?"

She paused. "What's that supposed to mean?"

He glanced at his children, then nudged her toward the entry, where they wouldn't be heard. "What is it with you Hollywood people? Isn't it enough that I'm bringing Melody in for the audition? Do you have such a big ego that you have to gloat over your accomplishments?"

"First of all, I'm not Hollywood. And secondly, I wasn't gloating," she declared hotly, her voice an angry whisper.

He made a sound of disbelief. "You took great pride in telling Annabelle that you had won."

"I didn't win anything!" she exclaimed. "Look, I've said I was sorry. I honestly didn't know you hadn't told her."

Despite his anger, she could see that same gleam in his eye that had been there earlier when he had almost kissed her. She wanted to be cool toward him, but the sight of that little lock of hair hanging down over his forehead and the blue of his eyes wouldn't allow it.

"What kind of person do you think I am?" Her eyes begged for understanding.

He sighed and ran a hand through his hair. "One who's too good-looking for words. That's what the problem is."

"Now I need to apologize for my looks?"

He didn't answer, but stared at her. Kika thought she could almost hear the wheels clicking inside his head as a mental debate went on.

She didn't want to argue with him. "I think it's time I go." She was about to step out the door when he stopped her by placing a hand on her arm. "Why *did* you come over here tonight?"

"Right now I'm asking myself that same question," she murmured as she left.

SLEEP WAS NOT going to happen, Nick decided as he glanced at the digital clock next to his bed. It was one-fourteen. He supposed he could get up and take another cold shower. He knew, however, that that would not make him forget Kika Mancini.

He turned on the lamp and reached for the murder mystery on his nightstand. He had read for about an hour before he had turned off the light and he still wasn't done with chapter one.

That was because he couldn't get the picture of Kika in his denim shirt out of his mind. When she had handed him her wet T-shirt and the bra had fallen to the floor, he'd had all sorts of vivid images of what lay beneath his denim shirt. Although Beth had been taller than Kika, her bras were smaller.

He groaned. That was what this was all about: Kika's physical attributes. He was responding to her in a way any man would respond to a sexy woman.

It was all physical, he told himself. He was an adult male who hadn't been with a woman for a very long time. It didn't mean that he needed to get emotionally involved with Kika. It just meant that nature was letting him know he was alive.

But that bothered him. He didn't want to have any feelings—physical or emotional. He wanted to be numb. The day Beth died he had decided that fate had destined he would live without the comfort of a woman at his side.

After all, Beth had died because of him. He couldn't possibly enjoy himself with another woman. And he had nearly made the mistake of thinking that he could.

No more. Kika Mancini would be gone in a short while and he would forget that his body had ached for hers. He'd forget the way she looked holding Melody on her lap. He would forget the way her smile made him want to reach out and stroke her hair.

Even though everything about her turned him on, he had no room for any woman in his life. He flipped open the paperback and read the grisly details of a serial murder. It didn't help. He still saw Kika sitting in his denim shirt at the kitchen table with Melody on her lap.

CHAPTER TEN

AFTER THE EPISODE at the Miller home, Kika expected that Melody wouldn't be at the audition. Kika hadn't seen Nick since the evening he had dumped a bucket of water on her head...and that suited her just fine. She had been thinking about the man far too often in the past week, when what she needed to focus on was her work.

She had spent the weekend completing arrangements for the audition, checking on last-minute details with the film crew and working with Wendy to make sure everyone was aware of the time schedule.

By the time the toddlers began arriving at the school gym, a black velvet curtain provided the backdrop for a set that consisted of two rockers—one adult-size and one child-size. Wendy had each of the parents fill out an application and a consent form, then she sent them to Bob, a photographer who took an instant photo of the child, which Wendy attached to the application. Next Kika conducted the interview, which was videotaped—a familiar procedure, since she had already conducted thousands of interviews in Minneapolis.

If Kika thought moving the auditions to Tyler would make them less stressful, she was wrong. As had happened whenever she worked with small children, there were countless delays with the taping. A child would have a temper tantrum, one would need a diaper change, another one wouldn't sit still long enough to get a picture taken. Then there were those who cried during the entire process.

One noticeable difference, however, was the lack of stage moms. So far, not one parent had campaigned shamelessly or attempted to bribe Kika for the chance at stardom.

During lunch break, Kika compared notes with her assistant, Wendy. They had arranged to have food brought to the school rather than sit in Marge's Diner. Eating egg salad sandwiches at a folding table in a quiet room was better than feeling like guppies in a fish bowl, which was how Kika felt in the small town.

"We're never going to get through the list if we don't pick up the pace," Wendy commented as she handed Kika a cup of coffee.

Kika removed the plastic lid and took a sip. "You think I'm spending too much time with each one?"

"At the rate we're going, we'll probably run out of tape."

"I thought I told you to expect two hundred." Kika cast an accusing eye at her assistant.

"You did, but I thought we could weed out the ones we know aren't going to work," Wendy explained.

Kika regarded her suspiciously. "What are you suggesting?"

"I could cue you for the ones who don't have what it takes. Then you could cue Dan and he could just pretend to be taping." Dan was the technician behind the camera, a seasoned pro Kika had worked with often. "Remember when we did that for the diaper commercial?"

"Yes, but that was in the city," Kika reminded her.

"So?" Wendy gave her a blank look.

"So, many of these parents have been unemployed for the past six months because of a fire to the big industry in town."

"What does that have to do with us not taping their kids?" Wendy leaned forward, her shirt coming dangerously close to her egg salad. "If you know they're not going to work out anyway, what's the point?"

Before coming to Tyler, Kika would have agreed with her assistant. There had been times when she hadn't wanted to tell parents to their faces that their child didn't have what it took to be a star. Pretending to be taping seemed the least painful way to reject them. Now, however, it seemed misleading.

"I really don't like the idea," Kika protested.

"We're way over budget on this project already," Wendy reminded her.

Kika knew what she said was true. And if they could eliminate some of the kids right at the start, she wouldn't have to sit and watch endless feet of video of children who were totally inappropriate for the job.

"Dan, what do you think?" Wendy drew the cameraman into the debate.

"I'm with Wendy on this one," he told Kika. "If we're going to finish up here today, we're going to have to cut to the chase."

Kika chewed on her lower lip. As much as she hated to admit it, she knew it was true. Against her better judgment, she worked out a system of hand signals. A closed fist meant forget the tape. An open palm meant go for it.

Since they were running an hour behind schedule, Kika hurried through lunch. Before opening the doors to the next batch of hopefuls, she washed down two aspirins with a soda. Because she was staying at the lodge out of town, she had been able to avoid running into Nick. But as Melody's name moved closer to the top of the audition list, Kika's stomach began to churn. Would the little redhead show up for her appointment?

To Kika's surprise, she did. Only it wasn't Nick who brought her, but Glenna McRoberts. In her arms Melody clutched the white bear with the purple ribbon around its neck.

"How's it going?" the day-care teacher asked Kika while Melody had her picture taken.

"It's been a long day," Kika confessed, glancing at her watch. "I can't believe it's after six."

"Nick had to work late so I offered to bring Melody to the audition," she told Kika.

"Thank you." Kika smiled warmly. Although there was no need for the hand signals, Wendy flashed Kika a wide-open palm, which Kika in turn flashed to Dan.

Just as expected, Melody didn't say a word during the audition. She sat in the small wooden rocker, the white bear scrunched in beside her, and smiled in such an adorable fashion that Kika had to resist the urge to pull her onto her lap and hug her.

When it was over, Melody didn't want to leave. She clung to Kika's long skirt, until finally Glenna had to pry her little fingers loose.

From then on, Kika was distracted. They continued taping—or not taping—until eight o'clock. At that point she was forced to tell those still waiting that she was sorry, but they were running behind schedule. Auditions would be completed in the morning.

For those parents who worked and couldn't bring their children in during the day, Kika offered to be there in the evening, as well. It would mean one more day in Tyler, but she figured it would be worth it. Besides, she wanted to talk to Nick before she went back to Minneapolis.

She debated whether she should go see him or simply pick up the phone. She chose to speak to him in person.

When taping was completed the following evening, she drove over to the Miller house. It was dark except for one light glowing in a second-story window. Kika didn't climb out of her car immediately, but sat contemplating what she would say to him.

Finally, she walked up to the front door and pressed the doorbell, her heart pounding in her chest. She wanted to see Nick, yet didn't want to see him. After what seemed like a very long time, a light came on in the living room and then the front door swung open.

Nick stood there in a pair of cutoffs and a T-shirt. He didn't bother to hide his surprise.

"I'm sorry to drop over so late, but I wanted to thank you for letting Melody come to the audition," Kika said a bit nervously.

He pushed open the screen door and gestured for her to step inside. "Cece's the one you should be thanking. It was her idea."

"Melody did very well. She wasn't the least bit shy," Kika said, a smile spreading across her face at the memory.

"She likes being with you."

The disappointment in his voice chased her smile away. Kika tried not to be offended, but his attitude only added to her feelings of inadequacy concerning the toddler. Did he dislike her that much or did he just think she would be a bad influence on a child?

"Well, you don't need to worry about it. If she's anything like her father, she'll forget about me in a few days," she said flippantly.

His eyes darkened. "I haven't forgotten about you, Kika."

The desire on his face told her he wasn't lying. She wanted to say something, anything, but her mouth had gone dry.

She licked her lips, not thinking of the provocative message it sent. "I—I'd better go. It's late and—"

She didn't get to finish. He pulled her into his arms and kissed her with a hunger that echoed what she had seen on his face. Her lips parted under his, inviting intimacy.

"I'm not a fickle man, Kika," he said when he finally lifted his mouth from hers. "I've wanted you since the moment I saw you at the airport, and that hasn't changed." His eyes held hers. "I'm not sure it ever will."

"And is that bad?" she asked with a wanton smile, her hands moving up inside his T-shirt. Before he could answer, she kissed him, a slow, drugging kiss that unleashed a passion in both of them.

His fingers found the buttons on her shirt, then the front clasp of her bra. Kika sighed with delight as a cool hand cupped her warm flesh.

"I like it when you touch me, Nick," she said in a throaty whisper. "Do you like it when I touch you?" Her hands traveled the length of his back until they reached the waistband of his shorts. There they parted. One slipped a finger through a belt loop, the other slid around to the front and palmed his fly.

Nick shuddered and closed his eyes.

He was so still Kika thought she had done something wrong. "Do you want me to go?"

He opened his eyes then, and what Kika saw made her tremble.

"No, I don't want you to go," he said, his breath hot against her face. "I want you to stay so I can show you that I know how to have fun."

"And how do you plan to do that?" she asked with a provocative push of her hips against his.

For an answer he lifted her in his arms. He carried her to a room Kika had discovered when she'd been searching for the laundry. It was a bedroom, but except for a small nightstand and a bed with a green-and-blue-plaid comforter, there was no other furniture.

By the light of a small ginger-jar lamp, he slowly undressed her. After dropping each article of clothing, he planted a kiss—on her mouth, on her neck, on her breast, on her thigh.

While his lips made every tender spot on her body tingle with anticipation, Kika thought she would die with longing. He must have been thinking along the same lines. Before she knew it, his naked body was beside hers on the bed, pulling her to him with an intensity of emotion that was both exciting and frightening.

She forgot all the reasons she wasn't supposed to get involved with him. He wasn't the father of three children. He wasn't a mechanical engineer who lived in Wisconsin. He was simply the man she wanted to feel inside her. The man she needed to make love with. The man who could take away the terrible ache that made nothing seem important except being loved by him.

Kika had often heard from friends that it was possible to want nothing from a man but sex. Until she met Nick, she hadn't believed it. Now she wasn't so sure. With an abandonment totally unfamiliar to her, she responded to his touch, matching kiss for kiss, lifting her hips to coincide with the rhythm of his body.

He filled her senses completely, giving her a pleasure she had never known before. Every helpless sound he emitted had her pulling him closer to her until she felt as if they were one. Nothing could stop their passion. As she savored every moment of ecstasy, her only wish was that it would never end.

With an incredible joy it did end. They lay side by side, basking in the afterglow of their passion, and Kika realized that never before had she felt so alive, so cherished or so satiated.

She looked at the man responsible for her euphoria and said, "I can't believe I ever accused you of not knowing how to have fun."

Nick propped himself up on one elbow and stared down into her eyes. "That wasn't fun, Kika."

The glow began to fade. When she would have turned her head away from him, he placed a hand along her jaw.

"That was uncontrollable desire," he told her, his eyes brimming with emotion. He placed butterfly kisses on her forehead, her nose and her mouth. Then, with slow deliberation, he began to caress her swollen breasts.

"Fun is what comes next," he said with a devilish grin.

KIKA AWOKE the following morning to find herself alone in the double bed. The only clothes on the floor were hers. Hearing sounds in other parts of the house, she quickly scrambled out of bed and dressed.

As she crossed the hallway to the bathroom, the aroma of freshly brewed coffee teased her nostrils. She could hear dishes clanging and children's voices.

What time had Nick left her bed? She warmed at the memory of the night they had spent together. It had been so wonderful falling asleep in his arms. She only wished that she could have found him beside her when she awakened.

When she had finished washing up, she did her best to comb her hair and fix her face. Using her finger, she applied toothpaste to her teeth and scrubbed as best she could. As she stared in the mirror she expected to look different than she had yesterday. Last night had changed her.

When she opened the bathroom door, Melody was standing outside, a pink-and-white sunsuit covering her satiny smooth skin. On her feet were a pair of white sandals. Seeing Kika, she grinned.

"Hi, Melody." Kika returned the smile. The toddler followed her into the kitchen.

There Kika found Nick, dressed in a white shirt and a dark patterned tie, dress slacks and black leather shoes. He was setting a box of cereal and two bowls on the table. On the stove was a frying pan with a half-cooked piece of French toast in it.

When he saw Kika, his eyes darkened. She wanted him to give her a kiss and a smile. He didn't. He simply said, "There's fresh coffee over there." He used the pancake turner to gesture toward the coffee maker on the countertop.

Uncomfortably aware of the fact that she was wearing yesterday's blouse with a spaghetti stain on the sleeve, Kika muttered, "Thanks," and went to pour herself a cup. She wished he would say something about last night.

Just then Patrick and Zachary breezed into the kitchen.

"Hi, Kika! Dad says you slept over last night but we can't tell Grandma," Patrick said.

Kika shot Nick an inquisitive glance.

He quickly looked away, as if embarrassed. Kika wondered if he was already regretting what had happened between them.

"Boys, just sit down and eat your cereal or you're going to make us all late." Nick flipped the French toast, then put Melody in her high chair.

"How come you slept overnight?" Patrick asked, which prompted his brother to elbow him.

"You're not supposed to ask questions, remember?" Zachary reprimanded him.

"No, it's all right," Kika answered, sitting down at the table next to the boys. She ignored the warning she saw in Nick's eyes. "You see, I came to see your dad last night because I wanted to talk to him about Melody's interview. I had worked a really long day and I was too tired to drive all the way back to the lodge, so your dad let me use the guest bedroom," she explained.

She heard Nick breathe a sigh of relief.

"Oh," Patrick replied. "Can you sleep over again tonight? Then you can play games with us. Tonight is game night."

"I'm afraid I have to go back to Minneapolis this afternoon."

"You're leaving today?" Nick looked surprised.

She nodded. "My work here is finished. I have to go back and show the tapes to Mr. Fancy." She glanced at the clock and realized that Wendy was probably wondering where she was. "I didn't realize it was so late. Could I use your phone?"

Nick nodded. "Be my guest."

She dialed the lodge and asked for Wendy's room, but there was no answer. "I hope she's not worried about me," Kika commented as she put the phone back on the hook. "I should have called and told her I wouldn't be back last night."

Again Nick shot her an uneasy look.

"I'd better go," she said uneasily.

"Aren't you going to eat any breakfast?" Patrick asked as she headed toward the back door.

"I can't right now." How could she stay when Nick was treating her as if she were an embarrassment? All she could think about was getting away. "You boys will have to eat my share," she said, then hurried off.

Nick made no attempt to stop her. There was a sound of protest, however, as she disappeared out the door.

"No!"

It came from Melody's lips. Her father and brothers stopped and stared at her.

"Did she say no?" Nick asked his sons.

"I think she did, Dad," Zachary answered.

"Melody, do you want Kika to go home?" Nick asked.

"No." It was only one word, and then her lips were shut again.

"Hey, Mel, do you want some peas?" Zachary asked.

"No."

"What about spinach?" Patrick added.

"No."

Nick flipped a piece of French toast onto her plate. "How about some French toast?"

She nodded and the boys sighed.

"HERE'S THE LIST." Kika handed her assistant a sheet of paper.

"You're calling back five for Fancy's Baby?" Wendy looked at her skeptically. "I thought you only wanted the Miller kid."

"I do, but there's no guarantee we're going to get her. Any one of those five would work."

"I can't believe you're saying that." Wendy stared at her boss in disbelief. "What happened to 'If I don't get the perfect baby my career is over'?"

"It's just another job, Wendy. And I really do believe any of those five would work."

"What does Fancy think?"

"I'm not showing him the tapes until we've done the callbacks." Kika shuffled some papers on her desk and changed the subject, not wanting to admit that she was afraid Melody wouldn't be the baby Fancy would choose. "Call all the parents except Melody's. I'll take care of her."

"I don't suppose that would have anything to do with the fact that she has a hunk for a father?" Wendy teased.

Kika hadn't brought her sense of humor to work. "Wendy, my private life is my own business," she snapped, then turned her attention to her PC.

"Sorry," Wendy retorted in an offended tone.

Kika rubbed her temples. "No, I'm the one who's sorry. This assignment has stressed me to the max. I feel like I don't know what I'm doing, that my judgment is totally off center."

"It's been a busy summer. Starsky called to say he needs those extras for that hockey movie by next Monday."

Kika wrinkled her face. "Just what I need—to work three days straight without sleep."

"Hey, it's a feature film. You're the one always says the feature is everything."

"I know. I guess I'm just tired." Kika got up from her desk and walked over to the window. Through the tinted glass she could see Lake Calhoun. It always amazed her that no matter what the time of day, there was always activity surrounding the city lake. Joggers, walkers, bicyclists and in-line skaters competed for space on the pavement, while sunbathers and swimmers vied for spots on the sand.

At the sight of a mother pushing a stroller, Kika's heart skipped a beat. She watched as the woman spread a blanket on the ground, then released her little girl from the stroller and set her down to play in the sand.

"What are you staring at?" Wendy asked.

That brought Kika back to reality. "People. Doesn't anybody work? That beach is always crowded."

"It's summer. Kids are out of school." Wendy handed her a manila folder. "Here's the final expense report for the Tyler trip. What day are we doing the callbacks?"

"Next Friday," Kika answered. "That ought to give everyone sufficient notice to make arrangements."

It would also give her enough time to convince Nick that Melody should make the trip to Minneapolis. Kika knew it wasn't going to be easy. If only there wasn't that sex thing hanging in the air between them.

"NICK, YOU HAVE a call on line one—an Annabelle Scanlon."

The first thought that went through Nick's head as he reached for the phone was that one of the kids was sick. Why else would his mother-in-law call him at work?

"What is it, Annabelle?"

"Have they called you about Melody?"

"Has who called me?" he asked, his anxiety increasing by the moment. "Is she sick?"

"No, I'm talking about the movie people. Three of the little girls from TylerTots have already been told they made the callbacks. It's all over town. I thought they might have called you."

He heaved a sigh of relief. "I haven't heard anything."

"Do they have your work number?"

"Yes."

This time Annabelle was the one to sigh in relief. "Then she must not have made it. All the others were called first thing this morning."

Nick experienced a pang of disappointment. It was odd that he should feel badly about something he was opposed to in the first place, but he supposed it was only natural. After all, Melody had grown fond of Kika Mancini. This meant they wouldn't see her again—either one of them.

While Annabelle rambled on about how it was for the best that Melody hadn't been chosen, Nick doodled on a scratch pad at his fingertips. By the time he hung up the phone, he had written "Kika" four times.

Out of sight, out of mind, he told himself as he drove home that evening. Only his heart didn't listen. How could it? He was finally able to start a day with a feeling of optimism instead of regret. Unfortunately, the person responsible for that brightness was a woman he needed to forget.

That was why he came to the conclusion that Melody's not making the callbacks for Fancy's Baby was for the best. His sons didn't agree, however. The first thing Zachary said when Nick picked him and Patrick up from Adventure Club was, "Melody's not going to be Fancy's Baby, is she?" The same disappointment Nick had felt earlier in the day was now evident on his sons' faces.

"I guess not," Nick answered.

"Why not? She's just as cute as Brian Bartlett's little sister," Zachary insisted.

"Grandma says being on TV ruins a kid anyway," Patrick added.

"Well, it's nothing we need to worry about, is it?" Nick stated philosophically. "How about if we stop at the Dairy King and pick up hamburgers and fries for supper?"

No sooner had the paper wrappers and plastic cups been tossed in the trash half an hour later than the telephone rang. Since Nick was busy wiping chocolate milkshake from his daughter's fingers, Zachary answered the phone.

"Oh, hi." Nick could only hear his son's end of the conversation. "He's here, but he's washing Melody's hands."

Nick wanted to ask who was calling, but Melody was whining, upset that he had removed several cold, hard french fries from her tray before she had finished with them. All he could hear was Zachary saying, "Uh-huh," followed by an "Umm-hmm."

Then he heard his son let out a whoopee. "She made it!" He held the phone away from his ear and looked at Nick. "Hey, Dad! Melody made the callbacks for Fancy's Baby."

Nick dropped the washcloth on the table and went to take the phone. The sound of Kika's voice on the other end made his insides tingle.

"Nick, is that you?"

"Yes." He wanted to say more, but all he could think about was how she had looked lying naked in his arms. He glanced at his sons to see if they had a clue about his thoughts. Of course they didn't, and he let his shoulders relax.

"I guess Zachary has already told you the news," Kika said with that wonderful little giggle he had come to love. "I hope you're pleased."

At the moment he had mixed feelings about Melody's success. On the matter of seeing Kika again, however, he had no doubt. He was pleased at the prospect.

"The boys are excited," he told her, not wanting to admit his own feelings.

He cast another glance at his sons, who were jumping up and down, saying, "We're going to be rich."

Placing his palm over the mouthpiece, Nick said, "Be quiet."

"We need to talk about what happens next," Kika told him.

"I'm listening," he said coolly, trying not to sound too enthusiastic about seeing her again.

"There are five little girls scheduled for a second interview next week."

Nick glanced at the calendar on the wall. "What day?"

"We've booked the soundstage for Friday morning. We figured it was better to avoid nap times if possible."

"The soundstage?"

"We're going to hold this audition at a soundstage here in the Twin Cities."

"You want us to come to Minnesota?" His heart sank in his chest.

"It has to be that way. We can't do the kind of taping we need to make the final decision unless we're at a soundstage."

He closed his eyes briefly and sighed. "Then I'm afraid you'll have to do it without Melody. I just started a new job. I can't miss a day to take my daughter to an audition for a TV commercial."

Hearing his words, the boys groaned in unison.

"That's why I scheduled it for Friday. Zachary said you have every Friday off."

"Normally I do, but I've been assigned to a special project. I've already agreed to go in that day."

Kika groaned. "There must be some way we can work this out," she said hopefully.

"I don't see how. There isn't anyone who can travel with her that great of a distance."

"What if I brought her?" Kika offered.

Her suggestion caught him by surprise. "You're willing to come get her and take her back with you?"

Kika couldn't give up. "It would work, Nick. I could fly out and get her on Thursday evening, then bring her back home on Friday. It's only about an hour's flight."

"I couldn't ask you to do that," he said.

"Why not?"

"It's too big a responsibility. Who'd take care of Melody when you're working?"

There was a silence, and Nick could see that her offer had been an impulsive one.

"I could get my sister-in-law Frannie to watch her. She has a little boy about the same age."

"I don't think that's a good idea."

"You wouldn't have to worry about Frannie's credentials. I can vouch for her."

"That's not why I'm hesitating."

"You don't trust me?" There was a vulnerability in her voice that made Nick want to reassure her.

"Yes, I do trust you. It's just that Melody's not even two years old. You must understand why I have reservations about this."

In the background he could hear Zachary and Patrick encouraging him to "do it." Again, he put his hand over the mouthpiece, this time saying, "Go in the other room—both of you."

As soon as they were out of the kitchen, he asked Kika, "Does this mean that the commercial will have to be filmed in the Twin Cities as well?"

She cleared her throat, then said, "Yes, but all of your expenses will be paid."

"It's not the expense I'm worried about."

"It's the time away from your job. Yes, I understand that. You must know I'd do whatever I could to accommodate you."

Immediately Nick thought about all the wonderful things she could do to accommodate him. None of them had to do with the audition.

"Why don't you let me think about this?" he suggested.

"Okay. Why don't you call me this weekend?"

"That would be fine," he told her, not wanting at that moment to tell her no. Maybe it would get easier to turn down her offer if he couldn't hear her honeysweet voice on the phone. Right now, every nuance in her tone made him think about their one night together, preventing him from speaking logically on any subject.

Only Nick didn't turn down her offer. As each day passed, he thought he'd fax her a quick message, declining her invitation. He told himself it was because he didn't want to pass up an opportunity for Melody to earn money for college and that the boys would be disappointed if their sister didn't get a chance to be on television. Deep down in his heart, however, he knew there was more to it than his sons' disappointment and his daughter's college fund. This was an opportunity to see Kika again. To have her in his house, to try to convince her that what had happened between them wasn't simply a fleeting thing.

One question burned a hole in his curiosity: did she want to see him again, too, or was she just interested in making money off his daughter?

CHAPTER ELEVEN

"DON'T LOOK NOW, but the guy at the end of the bar is trying to get your attention," Lucy told Kika as they ate lunch in a bistro in downtown Minneapolis.

Kika didn't bother to turn her head but simply stared at the Caesar salad in front of her. "I'm not interested."

"He looks like Andy Garcia."

Kika shrugged. "If that's the case he won't have any trouble getting a woman's attention."

"He's having trouble getting yours." Lucy lifted her coffee mug, peering at her niece over its rim. "Aren't you even curious to see what he looks like?"

"No. I'm too tired to care."

The coffee mug landed on the table with a thud. "Since when have you been too tired to notice a perfect tush squeezed into tight denim?"

Kika shrugged. "I don't know. Maybe I've seen too much denim-covered tush in the past two years." She pushed the romaine lettuce around with her fork.

"If you keep poking at that lettuce you're going to have soup, not salad."

Kika set her fork down and shoved her plate aside. She turned her attention to her glass of soda, swirling the clear liquid aimlessly.

"Wendy said George Loken's going to hire you for his next film," Lucy remarked.

Kika sighed. "It's another basketball movie. I'm not sure I should tackle such a big project."

"Why not?"

"He needs to fill the Target Center with fans."

"You had the whole ice arena packed with extras for that hockey movie. What's the problem?"

Again Kika shrugged. "There isn't one, I guess." She looked at her watch and frowned.

"Am I keeping you from an appointment?"

Kika reached over to give her aunt's hand a gentle squeeze. "No, I'm sorry. It's just that I'm expecting a phone call this afternoon."

"It must be an important one."

She took a sip of soda before saying, "It has to do with Fancy's Baby. I told you we've narrowed the field down to five, didn't I?"

"Really? That's great! Did you get the little red-head you wanted?"

"That's what the phone call's about. I'll know today whether it's yes or no." The prospect had Kika's stomach tied in knots.

"Is the father still having second thoughts?"

Kika jabbed at the ice cubes in her glass with her straw. "The problem is the location. He can't take any time off from his job. If he gives his permission, I'm going to have to go to Tyler and bring Melody back here for the taping."

"Isn't that a little bit above and beyond the call of duty?" Lucy asked with raised eyebrows.

"I don't mind."

Lucy bit the end off a carrot stick and pondered her statement thoughtfully. "Let me get this straight." She stabbed the remainder of the carrot in the air for emphasis. "You're going to fly to Wisconsin, pick up this little girl, bring her to the taping, then fly her back home again?''

Kika nodded. "Don't look at me like that. It's not what you think."

"Maybe you should tell me what's happening," Lucy urged in a maternal tone. "I have a feeling that, whatever it is, it's the reason you've lost your appetite and your interest in denim-covered tushes."

Kika groaned and ran her fingers through her hair. "Oh, Luce, I don't know what to say. Things just . . . happened when I was in Tyler."

"With the baby or with the father?"

She sighed. "Both."

"Do you want to talk about it?"

Kika stared into dark brown eyes that had always held understanding. Once again she saw compassion and concern. If there was one person she knew she could count on, it was Lucy.

"There's this strong sexual attraction between me and Nick Miller," she said quietly.

"Aha! So that's why you can't eat. You're in love."

"I didn't say I was in love," she retorted. "I said I was attracted to him."

"I've never known you to lose your appetite over a man."

"Probably because he's not like any man I've ever known."

Lucy tapped her acrylic fingernails on the table and rolled her eyes heavenward. "Where have I heard that one before?" Sensing Kika's indignation, she quickly added, "Okay, so you're attracted to this guy. Why is that a problem?"

"Lucy! He has three kids!"

"Most people would call that a blessing, not an incurable disease," she admonished gently.

Kika felt suitably chastised. "They're beautiful children—three little redheads. And they're smart. And self-sufficient. Of course, they've had to be, not having a mother."

Again Lucy studied her niece's pale features. "You don't just like him. You like his kids, too, don't you?"

She nodded miserably.

Lucy chuckled.

Kika didn't see the humor in the situation. "I thought you of all people would understand."

Lucy reached for her hand. "I do understand. That wasn't a funny laugh, it was an expression of gratitude. Don't you see? You're finally starting to let go of the past."

"Because I like Nick Miller's kids?"

"Because you've allowed yourself to get close enough to find out you like them," Lucy answered.

"But I don't want to be close to them," she insisted.

"Are you sure?"

Kika didn't respond. She couldn't. Fear wouldn't allow her to consider the answer to that question. She had accepted the fact that she would never be a mother. To open the door to the possibility that she could care for someone else's children meant taking a risk she wasn't prepared for.

"You haven't told me how this Nick Miller feels about you," Lucy commented.

"He thinks I'm terrible with children."

"That's not what I asked."

Kika looked down at her hands. "I don't know how he feels about me."

"Does he want to see you again?"

She shrugged. "That's why this phone call is so important."

"I thought you said the phone call was about Melody."

"It is."

Lucy reached across the table to give her niece's arm a comforting squeeze. "You want him to be calling about you, not his daughter, right?"

Kika nodded unhappily. "I doubt that will happen. I should just forget about him."

"Can you do that?"

Kika didn't answer.

"Tell me something. What frightens you more—your feelings for Nick or your feelings for his children?" Lucy asked.

It was a question Kika thought about often during the next few days. She didn't understand how Nick and his children could have become so important to her in such a short time. Of one thing she was certain. If she wasn't careful, she would lose something more important than Fancy's Baby. She would lose her heart.

KIKA FOUND Nick waiting for her when she stepped off the plane in Milwaukee on Thursday evening. He looked wonderfully familiar, with his dimpled grin and the lock of hair that refused to stay back off his forehead. He stood against the waiting-room wall, as if he didn't have a care in the world, his tie loose around his neck and his suit coat slung over his shoulder.

"I didn't expect to see you here," she said as he reached for her overnight bag.

"Since I was already in town I thought I might as well meet your plane. Have you had dinner?"

"No."

"Want to join me?"

"Sure, but what about your kids?"

"Annabelle's with them. They'll be fine."

As they made their way through the terminal to the parking lot, they talked as if they were old friends. During dinner at a restaurant on the outskirts of Milwaukee, his attitude didn't change. He treated her as if she were a friend who would be taking care of his daughter for the next twenty-four hours, not the woman he had made passionate love to one hot summer night.

It was only when they were seated in the convertible with the stars shining overhead that the atmosphere changed. As he drove the interstate between Milwaukee and Tyler, Kika became aware of the glances he cast in her direction. Gone was the friendly twinkle, replaced by a hooded desire that sent a tremor of longing through her.

Gradually, conversation became more stilted. By the time they reached Tyler's city limits, all talk had stopped. Nick pulled off the highway into the parking lot of a gas station that had already closed for the night. He steered away from the one lonely street lamp burning dimly on the corner.

"Is something wrong?" she asked as he killed the car's engine.

"There are things I want to say to you and I don't exactly want to be saying them sitting out front of Granny Rose's," he answered.

"What things?" she asked.

"This for one." He leaned across the seat and pulled her into his arms, covering her mouth with his. It was the kind of kiss Kika had wanted him to give her when she had stepped off the plane. Full of passion, it said that he had missed her just as much as she had missed him.

When it ended they were both breathing heavily. He rested his forehead against hers and fought for self-control.

"As much as I'd like to continue this, I don't think a Mustang convertible is the best place for this type of conversation." He straightened, brushing a wisp of blond hair back from her face. "The boys wanted you to stay at the house with us."

"And what did you want?"

He released her and leaned back in his seat. "I can't have what I want, Kika."

"Why don't you tell me and let me be the judge of that?" She reached over and began toying with the buttons on his shirt.

He captured her fingers in his hand, then brought them to his lips. "I'm sorry about the way things ended between us."

"Are you sorry that I left or sorry that I spent the night?" She held her breath as she waited for his answer.

"The only regret I have about that night is that it was over before we had a chance to talk about it." He didn't release her hand, but held it tightly within his two large ones.

"You acted as though you didn't have anything to say in the morning," she reminded him.

"You didn't hang around long enough to find out."

"Because I thought you didn't want me there. You wouldn't talk to me."

"I wasn't sure what to say. I don't make a habit of sleeping with women I've known only a week."

"Is that all it was? A week?" she asked wistfully. "It felt as though we knew each other longer than that."

"Yes, it did," he agreed.

"There's such a strong physical attraction between us," she said quietly. "It's never happened to me like this before—so fast and so intense."

"Me neither." He reached across to stroke her cheek with the back of his fingers. "I guess that's why I didn't know what to say to you when you came waltzing into the kitchen looking so normal."

"How was I supposed to look?"

"I liked the way you looked. It's just that I could barely get dressed that morning and here you were bouncing into the kitchen as if you hadn't stayed awake half the night making..." He paused, as if suddenly unsure what to call their night of passion.

"We made love," she supplied quietly.

He stared out over the steering wheel, as if searching in the darkness for his next words. After what seemed like an eternity of silence, he asked, "Isn't it a little too early to call it that?"

"I'm not sure," she admitted honestly. "All I know is that it was too important to pretend it didn't happen."

He looked at her then with heavy-lidded eyes and said, "I want it to happen again."

Then he pulled her close, settling his mouth on hers in a hungry kiss that made her go limp in his arms. His hand sought her breast and she shivered with delight, forgetting everything but the exquisite sensation of his touch.

Nick would have liked to forget everything but the sweetness of her lips, but he knew that no matter how much he wanted to spend the night with Kika, he couldn't. He had three kids waiting for him at home. With a supreme effort, he lifted his head and removed his hand.

"It kills me to have to say this, but I have to take you to Granny Rose's. I promised Annabelle I wouldn't be late," he told her, trying not to succumb to the temptation to kiss her one more time.

Although she nodded her head in understanding, a tiny sigh escaped her lips. Nick couldn't resist planting one last kiss on her mouth.

They rode in silence for several minutes before he said, "I'd like you to spend the weekend in Tyler."

"Want to have more fun, Nick?"

He shot her a sideways glance and saw that same flirtatious look she had given him the first night they had met. "Can you get away for the weekend?"

"I think so. Will it cause a problem with Annabelle?"

"No."

"You sound awfully certain about that."

He wasn't, but he didn't want to think that anything could go wrong with his plans to be with her. "Don't borrow trouble," was what his grandmother had always said, and right now he understood the wisdom of her words.

"Annabelle has a good heart. She just has to get used to seeing me with someone other than Beth," he told her, ignoring the little voice in his head that said he, too, struggled with the same problem. Ever since he had felt the first stirrings of attraction for Kika, a part of him had protested, made him feel disloyal. For so many years Beth had been the only woman he'd needed, the only woman he'd wanted.

"I'm sure I can stay at the lodge if Granny Rose's is filled," Kika told him.

Nick knew that there was only one place he wanted her to stay and that was with him. Yet he couldn't say that. Not because he worried about what Annabelle would think, but because he was afraid that if Kika moved in with him for even two days he wouldn't want to let her go again. They needed more time before they made that decision.

"I promised the boys I'd take them swimming during the day, but I can probably get a sitter for Saturday night," he told her as he turned onto Main Street.

"You want me to bring my swimsuit?"

Images of the string thing with the green triangles popped into his head and caused a certain part of his anatomy to throb. "Do you want to come swimming with us?"

"Sure, but I don't want to intrude on your family time."

He thought it was a strange thing for her to say. Did she really worry that she would be intruding or was it that she really didn't want to be around his children?

It was an issue he would have liked to explore, but as he pulled up in front of Granny Rose's Bed-and-Breakfast, Joe and Susannah Santori were sitting out on the porch. Any opportunity for private conversation was gone.

A short time later, as Nick drove home, doubts began to creep into his thoughts. Maybe he was only fooling himself to think that someone like Kika would want to be a part of his life—a life that included three kids. She had told him right from the start that she had no intention of being a traditional wife and mother. Although she seemed to get along with the boys, he couldn't help but wonder if that wasn't part of her sales pitch as a casting director. She was used to getting people to do what she wanted.

As he pulled the Mustang into his drive, he could see Annabelle looking out the window. He only hoped she wasn't going to give him the third degree about this evening or launch into another sermon on why Melody shouldn't be Fancy's Baby.

To his surprise, his mother-in-law said nothing on either subject. Grateful, he thanked her for putting the kids to bed, kissed her cheek and said goodbye. The only awkward moment came when she reminded him of the barbecue.

"Barbecue?" He didn't remember her telling him she was planning any cookout.

"Yes. I've invited over some of the people of Tyler so you can get to know them. Elaine Jackson will be coming from Sugar Creek. She's a friend of Brick Bauer, the police chief."

"When is this barbecue?" he asked, feeling a sudden sinking sensation in his stomach.

"Why, Saturday, of course. See you then!" And with a wave she was gone.

Saturday. No. He would not give up his evening with Kika. He would simply have to tell Annabelle he was bringing a guest—Elaine or no Elaine.

Whenever he held Kika in his arms, Nick felt confident that they could make their relationship work. However, whenever they were apart, the doubts flooded in. The key was to not let her out of his sight.

His hopes for the weekend began to dim as the reality of the situation set in. He was falling in love with a woman who didn't like children and who lived two hundred and fifty miles away. What chance did they have to make a relationship work?

Early the next morning Nick dropped Zachary and Patrick at Adventure Club, then took Melody over to Granny Rose's to pick up Kika. Any apprehension he'd had concerning leaving Melody in Kika's care vanished when he saw the way his daughter's face lit up when Kika climbed into the car.

There was a bond forming between the two of them. He could sense it, and it gave him hope that Kika wasn't faking her devotion to his daughter.

As they entered the airport, he saw how capable and self-sufficient Kika was as she checked in at the airlines. With the ease of a seasoned traveler, she handed over her small suitcase and Melody's car seat, got boarding passes and seat assignments, making sure the flight attendants knew she was flying with a toddler. She was so different from Beth, who never would have stepped on an airplane by herself. She hadn't even liked going to the grocery story alone. But then Kika was a career woman, accustomed to being on her own. The thought brought a frown to his face, a frown that Kika misinterpreted as anxiety over Melody's trip.

"You can relax, Nick. I promise I'll take good care of her," she told him as they waited at the departure gate.

He smiled at the picture the two of them made standing side by side. Without knowing what Kika would be wearing, he had dressed Melody in a denim jumper and a white T-shirt, only to discover that Kika was wearing a similar outfit. As they waited in line to board the plane, they looked like mother and daughter.

It was a picture Nick wanted to carve in his memory, and it made him realize that he needed to confront feelings he had stifled. He didn't just want Kika for himself. He wanted her for his daughter.

All too quickly the announcement came for all passengers with small children to start boarding. Nick lifted Melody in his arms, hugging her close as he kissed her cheek. "You be good for Kika, okay?"

She shook her head and looked in Kika's direction, a big smile on her face.

"Do I get a kiss and a hug, too?" Kika gave him an appealing grin.

Still holding Melody, he leaned over and captured her mouth with his in a brief but sensuous kiss that hinted at what would happen when she came back for the weekend. When he would have released her, she reached up and pulled him close.

"I said a kiss and a hug," she whispered close to his ear, her breath hot on his flesh.

"We have a lot to talk about this weekend," he said as he handed over Melody and her bear.

"I'm looking forward to it." Kika gave him one last smoldering look that made him want to buy a ticket and get on the plane himself, then she headed for the departure gate.

He followed, standing to one side as they checked in with the flight attendant.

"This is a new experience for both of us. It'll be good for us," Kika told him, giving his arm a comforting squeeze.

As the two of them disappeared down the boarding ramp, Nick was overwhelmed with a sense of loss. He knew it was irrational. They were both coming back. Or were they? He knew that Melody would be with him again, but would Kika want to stay when she returned?

He pushed aside his doubts with a determined shake of his head. Kika was not the kind of woman to simply use him to get his daughter to star in a commercial. Her feelings for him ran as deeply as his did for her. All they needed was some time to get it straightened out.

This weekend. Saturday night, to be specific. He would take her to Annabelle's barbecue. And afterward... He drove to work with a gleam in his eye. Thank goodness it was Friday and he didn't have long to wait.

"THAT'S IT. I'm out of here, and not a moment too soon," Kika told Wendy as she threw several manila folders into her briefcase. They had finished taping the Fancy Baby auditions earlier and had spent the rest of the afternoon taking notes as they reviewed the tapes.

"I think the Miller kid's a shoo-in," Wendy commented as Kika slid her feet back into her shoes.

"She is good, isn't she?" Kika smiled reflectively.

"What would you have done if that Sweeney kid was better?"

"Gone with the Sweeney kid. Why?"

Wendy eyed her suspiciously. "Just wondering. You coaxed the little Miller kid a bit more than you did the others."

Kika shot her an indignant look. "I did not."

"It doesn't matter. She's perfect. If Fancy doesn't love her..." She threw her hands in the air.

"He will love her," Kika said confidently. "She's exactly what he asked for—cute, sweet, innocent and red-haired." She glanced at her watch. "I better hurry. I have to go pick her up at Frannie's and get to the airport."

"I thought you said your plane wasn't leaving until nine."

"It isn't, but I have a stop to make on the way."

The stop Kika made was at a toy store. After seeing the wonderful job Melody had done with the audition, Kika wanted to buy her something to play with on the plane going home. She found exactly what she was looking for in the section next to the dolls.

It was a plastic makeup kit complete with lipstick, powder compact and blush—all nontoxic and safe for children under three. Kika paid for her selection and hurried to her car.

Trying to get anywhere in the city on a Friday afternoon was a challenge. This rush hour was no different. A fender-bender on the freeway resulted in a thirty-minute drive taking close to an hour. By the time she arrived at Frannie's, what little patience she had was gone.

"I was worried you had had an accident. What happened?" Frannie asked as Kika hurried past her into the house.

"Traffic was awful. Where's Melody?"

"In with T.J. watching the video. I'll get her."

While Frannie was gone, Kika called the airline to confirm that their flight was on time. The traffic jam had slowed her down considerably, but she figured she could still make the flight as long as she didn't waste any time at Frannie's.

Melody smiled when she saw Kika. Without reservations, Kika scooped her up in her arms and planted a kiss on her cheek. At closer range she could see the little girl's eyes were puffy.

"What happened? Was she crying?" Kika looked at her sister-in-law as if she had committed child abuse.

"She and T.J. wanted the same truck," Frannie explained. "It was nothing."

"Nothing?" Kika echoed indignantly, giving Frannie another glare. To Melody she said in a soothing voice, "It's okay, Melody. Kika's here. We're going to get your things and go back on the airplane. Won't that be fun?"

The toddler smiled, until T.J. came barreling into the room with a truck in his hands, making motor sounds with his mouth. Seeing the possibility for another confrontation, Kika steered Melody away from her nephew.

Noticing the stuffed white bear sitting in a corner, she told her, "Go get your bear."

Before Melody had even taken a step in that direction, T.J. raced over to grab the toy. Upset that he had her prized possession, Melody wasted no time in going after him. The bear became the object of a tug-of-war. Frannie shouted, causing T.J. to let go. Startled, Melody flew backward, bumping her head on the floor. Within seconds, the tears began.

Kika rushed to her side. She gasped when she saw the stream of blood flowing from the little girl's mouth. "Frannie, look! She's bleeding!"

"She must have bit her lip when she fell." Calmly, Frannie lifted Melody into her arms and carried her to the bathroom. With a maternal calm she pressed a cold cloth to her mouth. "I think this should get looked at," she said, examining the cut on Melody's lip. "It might need stitches."

"Is it that bad?"

"I don't know, but we should have it checked just to be safe. We'll take her to emergency care." Frannie kept the cold cloth pressed against Melody's mouth as she carried her toward the front door.

"I'll drive," Kika said, holding the front door open.

"It'll be easier if we take my van. Here." Frannie handed her the little girl. "You hold her until I get T.J. strapped in, then we'll move Melody's car seat into the van."

Kika looked down at the beautiful little face which now looked as if she had been boxing with another toddler. Melody's entire lower lip was extended, swollen so badly Kika wondered why she wasn't crying.

The two-year-old was surprisingly calm. The tears had stopped. She simply looked at Kika with a helplessness that made her heart want to break in two.

I'll take good care of her. The promise Kika had made to Nick haunted her. She had let him down. In more ways than one, she realized as the true consequences of the accident sunk in. It just might be that she had put an end to any chance Melody had to be Fancy's baby.

NEVER WAS NICK SO anxious for a day to be over with than he was at five o'clock on Friday. Because Kika's plane wasn't arriving until after nine, he had accepted an invitation to have dinner with several of his co-workers. As he cleared his desk for the weekend, the phone rang. It was Annabelle.

"The boys want to know if they can order pizza for dinner." There was disapproval in her tone. Nick waited for the nutritional lesson to follow, but was surprised when it didn't come. She simply said, "What size should I get?"

"Better get a large," Nick answered. "Is everything okay?" He had a feeling that the pizza wasn't the only reason for Annabelle's phone call. He soon discovered he was right.

"Everything's fine. I hope Melody's all right."

"I'm sure she is," Nick said confidently.

"Well, I'm not so sure about that. I heard something today that disturbs me."

He sighed. He didn't want to know what she had heard if it was something critical of Kika, yet he found himself asking, "Are you talking about Kika?"

"She's dishonest, Nick. I know you don't want to hear that, but it's true. I have proof."

Against his better judgment he asked, "What proof?"

"She duped all those poor people who took time off from work to have their kids interviewed."

"Annabelle, what are you talking about?"

"I'm talking about how she wasn't even filming those kids. She was just pretending. Here are all these parents who go out and spend a lot of money on new clothes so their kids will have a shot at the modeling job and she doesn't even videotape them."

"I don't believe that, Annabelle."

She made a sound of disgust. "It's true. Ask Angela Murphy. She heard it from one of the mothers, who was there and saw it for herself. Miss Kika Mancini knew all along which babies she wanted." She clicked her tongue.

Nick was silent. What could he say? Until he talked to Kika, he wouldn't believe she could be a part of such a scheme.

"It was just a waste of time for those poor folks— and most of them couldn't afford it." Annabelle continued with her tirade.

He was losing his patience and knew he should hang up before he said things he'd regret. "Look, Annabelle, I really don't want to discuss this right now."

"Think about what I said," she advised him. "And we both better pray Melody's on that plane tonight."

This time he did lose his patience. "The woman's not a kidnapper, Annabelle."

"I wouldn't be so sure of that. Did you ever check out her credentials? I was watching one of those talk shows the other night and there was someone on there who had pretended to be a moviemaker when all he really wanted was to snatch people's babies from them."

"I have to go. I'm meeting some of the other employees here for dinner and they're waiting for me."

As soon as he was off the phone, Nick dialed the number on Kika's business card. He got her voice mail. "Hi, you've reached Mancini Casting Agency. We're either not in the office or unable to come to the phone. Please leave a message and we'll get back to you. Thanks."

He slammed the phone down and rested his hands in his head. What was wrong with him, listening to Annabelle's tabloid view of Kika? She would be on that plane and Melody would be safe, and Kika would tell him that she hadn't duped anybody.

He hoped.

CHAPTER TWELVE

BY THE TIME flight 705 landed, Nick had convinced himself that Kika had only slept with him to get Melody for the commercial. In his present state of mind, it seemed like a rational possibility. He conveniently forgot that he had already signed Melody up for the audition before he and Kika spent the night together.

He knew he was in an irrational state of mind—something he owed to Annabelle. If she hadn't planted such ugly rumors in his head he would never have suspected Kika could be dishonest about anything.

Wrong. A little voice in his memory bank contradicted him. Right from the start he hadn't trusted Kika, which was why he was having trouble discrediting the things his mother-in-law had said. He knew that people in show business would do anything to get what they wanted. But Kika was supposed to be different.

When people began to deplane, Nick's heartbeat accelerated. As passengers emerged from the jetway one by one, his chest tightened and he felt that familiar fluttering he always experienced whenever Kika was close by.

Only she wasn't close by—something he discovered as the last passengers from the flight slowly ambled away from the gate. When the doors to the jetway closed, Nick asked the attendant if there was anyone left on the plane. There wasn't.

He had an uneasy feeling in the pit of his stomach. Annabelle's words replayed in his memory: *We both better pray Melody's on that plane tonight.* He shook his head. Of course Kika would bring Melody back.

Thinking he must have had the wrong flight number, he stepped up to the ticket counter and inquired about the flights scheduled to arrive from Minneapolis.

"Are you Nick Miller?" the clerk asked. When he nodded, she added, "A Kika Mancini called to say she had missed her flight and that she would be arriving at ten forty-five." She handed him the piece of paper with the message.

Relief rolled over him. Of course Kika wasn't a kidnapper. He brushed the hair back from his forehead and sighed. He really was losing it. He went to a pay phone and called Annabelle to tell her he'd be late.

ALL THE WAY HOME Kika could think of one thing only: what would Nick think of her when he saw Melody's lip? "You'll have to buckle her into her own seat for the landing." The flight attendant's voice interrupted her musing. Eyes full of sympathy glanced first at Melody, then at Kika.

Kika looked down at the little girl sleeping in her arms and felt an emotion she had experienced only one other time in her life—when she had been pregnant with Caroline. Maternal instinct. She recognized it for what it was. Probably every woman felt those feelings when she held an adorable toddler in her arms. Kika didn't want to think that it was anything more than a natural reaction.

Carefully, she uncurled tiny fingers from her shirtsleeve, then slid her hands beneath chubby arms to lift Melody from her lap. She awoke with a start, looking lost and frightened.

"It's okay. I'm just going to move you next to me," Kika said softly. But Melody didn't want to leave the comfort of her arms. She protested loudly, her whole body stiffening as Kika tried to slide her into the next seat.

"Melody, you have to sit with the seat belt on so that the plane can go back on the ground and we can see your daddy." Kika tried to reason with her, but fatigue controlled the little girl's emotions, making her cranky and upset.

Tiny fists rubbed eyes clouded with tears. Kika could see the makings of a temper tantrum and carefully eased her back onto her lap.

"Please don't cry, Melody. You're going to make your lip hurt." She dabbed at the little girl's tears with a tissue, praying that the cut on her mouth wouldn't open. Melody continued to cry.

With the help of a flight attendant, and after much cuddling and coaxing, Kika eventually was able to get Melody to sit in her own seat with the safety belt fastened. The tears, however, didn't stop.

All during the landing, Melody sobbed quietly, her little shoulders shaking from the hiccups that accompanied the tears. Kika leaned over to put her arm around her, getting as close as her seat belt would allow. By the time the plane had landed and the announcement had been made that it was safe to leave,

Melody's face was puffy and red. Kika's apprehension increased.

It was bad enough that she was returning Nick's daughter with a fat lip. She didn't need to have Melody fussing as if she had been unhappy the entire trip.

Despite Kika's efforts to cheer her up, Melody refused to smile. Actually, she refused to do much of anything, which resulted in Kika having to carry her from the plane.

It was not an easy task. Besides Melody, she needed to carry the diaper bag, her briefcase, a shopping bag and her purse. In her haste, Kika didn't see that the white teddy bear had fallen under the seat.

The minute they stepped into the terminal, Kika spotted Nick. Looking more handsome than she remembered, he waved at her, causing her heart to skip a beat. He was happy to see her—it was there in his eyes, in the determined way he strode toward her and in his dimpled cheeks.

The smile, however, disappeared when Melody turned her head in his direction. Any welcome he planned to give Kika was lost—chased away by the sight of his daughter's distended lip.

"What happened?"

"I'm sorry," Kika said emotionally. "She was playing with my nephew and she fell. It's the reason why we're late. I had to take her to emergency care."

Nick didn't say a word, but lifted Melody into his arms, examining her face with an intense scrutiny.

"I tried to call you, but you had already left the office and no one knew where you were."

Kika wanted to reassure him. "The doctor said it looks worse than it is because the lip swells when it's been injured. There aren't any stitches so there shouldn't be any scarring.''

Nick tried to examine the cut, but Melody turned her face into his chest. Kika could only imagine what was going through his mind.

"She was quite brave at the doctor's office. And she was happy the entire flight except for when she had to be buckled in for the landing,'' she explained, her worst fears materializing as Nick continued to stare at her as if she were an incompetent employee instead of the woman he had taken to bed. "She's all right.''

As if contradicting her statement, Melody let out a wail.

Nick cradled his daughter in his arms, murmuring soothing words close to her ear. Melody continued to cry.

"I think she's tired,'' Kika suggested, shifting her briefcase and purse to the arm that had carried Melody.

"I'd like you to explain to me exactly what happened,'' he said as they stepped out of the stream of people heading for the exit.

Kika sensed an implied criticism. "Frannie said it was just one of those things. Even kids who have parents watching them play sometimes get hurt.''

"Where were you when this happened?''

"In the same room with her. It all happened so fast. Neither Frannie nor I had a chance to prevent it.''

Nick didn't ask any more questions, but simply said, "I better get her home.''

Kika was swamped with feelings of inadequacy. All she'd had to do was take care of one toddler for one day and she had botched the job.

Dejected, she followed Nick in silence to the baggage-claim area. He mumbled something about hoping the luggage handlers hadn't lost Melody's car seat. Kika murmured something about the claim ticket being in her purse.

By the time they reached the Mustang, Kika had made a decision. There was no reason for her to stay in Tyler for the weekend. She had thought she and Nick might have a future together, but today had pointed out how wrong she had been to dream any such thing could happen.

When Nick went to lift her overnighter into the trunk, she stopped him. "I'm not staying, Nick."

"Why not?"

"Because this isn't going to work."

He slammed the trunk shut with more force than was necessary. "No, I suppose it isn't. But then you never really wanted it to work, did you?" Anger flashed in his eyes.

"That's not true."

While they were arguing, Melody started to holler, a distressing call Nick couldn't ignore. He looked at Kika and said, "Look, you're not going to be able to catch a flight back tonight. Why don't I drop you off at a hotel?"

Knowing what he said was true, she reluctantly nodded, then climbed into the back seat of the Mustang. As soon as Nick had stowed her luggage in the trunk, he got in beside Melody and started up the car.

As they headed down the highway, the only sound in the car was Melody's wailing. It seemed to bother

Kika more than it did Nick. "Why is she crying?" she finally asked him.

"She's tired."

Kika wasn't convinced that was Melody's only problem. "She keeps looking around. Did we forget something?"

Nick glanced around the car. "She has everything she left with, doesn't she?"

It was then that Kika realized the white bear was missing. "Oh, no! We must have left her teddy bear on the plane. We're going to have to go back and see if we can find it."

"I'm not going back at this time of night. I'll call the airline tomorrow and tell them I'll stop in after work on Monday to pick it up," Nick said irritably. "Besides, she'll be sleeping in a few minutes."

If it had been up to Kika, she would have gone back to get the stuffed animal, but the longer they drove, the weaker Melody's crying became. Eventually she fell asleep.

Kika's eyes met Nick's in the rearview mirror. She needed to get away from him. She turned her attention to the billboards along the highway.

"There's a hotel coming up ahead. You can drop me off there," she suggested.

Again his eyes met hers, and she thought she saw desire flash briefly in them. But then he said, "Which exit is it?"

"Twenty-four."

They rode in silence for several minutes. As they approached the hotel, Kika could feel her time with him slipping away. She needed to set the record straight on one subject.

"You were wrong about what you said back at the airport, Nick. I did want this to work for us. I don't know why you would think I didn't."

"Maybe because you're so good at deceiving people," he told her.

She shook her head in disbelief. "What's that supposed to mean?"

"Don't look so innocent." Again their eyes met in the rearview mirror. "You duped half a town into believing their kids could be TV stars."

Hurt and confused she asked, "Why are you saying these things?"

"I know how you conduct your auditions—pretending to be videotaping when in reality nothing happens. What's the purpose, Kika? Do you get a kick out of exploiting innocent people?"

The derision in his voice robbed her of any desire to explain herself to him. He had been suspicious of her ever since they had met, and it was obvious that their night together hadn't convinced him that she could be anything more than a source of physical pleasure.

She remained silent until he had pulled into the parking lot of the hotel. "Just stop at the front door and I'll get a bellhop to take my suitcase in for me," she told him. If it hadn't been for Melody's car seat, she could have hopped out the front door. As it was, she had to wait for Nick to let her out his side.

With Melody asleep in the front seat and the bellhop waiting to take her suitcase, their parting was brief.

"Do you need a ride to the airport?" he asked.

She knew he was only being polite. "No, I can take the shuttle." She glanced at the little girl sleeping in the car and her heart contracted. "I'm really sorry about Melody's lip. I wish there was something I could do."

His look said it was too late to do anything.

She summoned her professional side and said, "I'll be in contact with you regarding the results of the interview."

His only response was a enigmatic lift of his eyebrows. Afraid she might embarrass herself by crying, Kika hurried into the hotel. She didn't look back.

TO NICK'S SURPRISE, it was after nine when he awoke the following morning. He found Zachary and Patrick in the living room watching Saturday morning cartoons. Except for a disinterested, "Hi, Dad," they paid him little attention as he passed through on his way to make his morning coffee.

While the coffee brewed, he decided to check on Melody. After their late night, he wasn't surprised that she wasn't up yet. Quietly he crept into her room. He found her sitting up in her crib playing with the white bear. Melody had taken the teddy bear to Minneapolis; Nick knew she had. Even Kika had said it was missing last night.

Nick scooped Melody up in his arms, bear and all, and carried her out to the living room, where he asked his sons, "Where did this come from?"

"Kika brought it over this morning."

Nick felt as if the bottom had fallen out of his stomach. Kika had been there and he hadn't seen her. She must have rented a car and driven all the way to Tyler simply to return Melody's bear.

"Why didn't you tell me she was here?" he asked in amazement.

"You were sleeping," Zachary answered.

Frustrated, Nick ran a hand through his hair. If he had known she was here they could have talked. Maybe they could have worked things out.

He shook his head. What was he thinking? She was the one who wanted to go back to Minneapolis. She had returned the bear without bothering to see him.

"She's not coming swimming with us today." If Zachary hadn't been only nine, Nick would have sworn there was an accusation in that statement.

"No, she had to go back to Minneapolis," Nick answered absently, his thoughts still on the fact that she had been at his house this morning and he had missed her.

"She said Melody's probably going to be Fancy's Baby," Zachary commented.

"Maybe," was all Nick said. He set Melody down on the floor next to the boys and went to get that cup of coffee.

"Kika?"

Nick stopped in his tracks. "What did she say?"

"She said Kika," Patrick answered.

Nick looked at his daughter and she giggled.

"Kika," she repeated, hugging the bear.

"So. Is HE bringing her or not?"

Kika pushed herself away from her desk and the probing eyes of her assistant. "I don't know. He hasn't returned my phone call yet." She walked over to the window and gazed out at Lake Calhoun.

The man in question was Nick Miller. Horace Fancy had agreed with Kika that Melody was the perfect baby to represent Fancy Furniture. Now all

Kika needed to do was arrange a meeting with Melody's father.

"You better hope he does. Baby number two is waiting in the wings and Fancy's not a patient man," Wendy warned.

Kika sighed. "I've done everything possible. There's nothing more I can do."

Wendy came up behind her and eyed her curiously. "That's the first time I've ever heard you say that."

"Say what?"

"That there's nothing more you can do."

"Well, there isn't."

"Are you sure? I don't know what's going on between you and this Nick Miller, but whatever it is, it's taken all the fight out of you."

"What am I supposed to do? Fly out there and drag him back here by his hair?"

"If that's what it takes. Come on, Kika. Where's that get-up-and-do-something attitude you've always had?"

Just then the phone rang. While Wendy went to answer it, Kika gazed out the window. As usual, there were lots of mothers with their children at the beach. Kika longed to be with them. She wanted to spread tropical-scented sunscreen on a little girl's fair skin, take her wading in the shallow water, build a sand castle on the beach. Of course, the little girl she had in mind was Melody Miller.

How could Kika have been so foolish as to think she could step into another woman's shoes and they would fit? Until she'd met Nick, fear had kept her from wanting to be a mother.

She sighed. Love did strange things to people. Love. It had given her hope that she could have it all—the husband, the kids and the white picket fence.

Where's your get-up-and-do-something attitude? Maybe Wendy had a point. There had been only a few times in Kika's life when she hadn't fought for what she wanted, and she had regretted them.

She wondered if this was going to be one of those times. The question was, what would she regret more—losing Fancy's Baby or losing Nick Miller?

NICK HAD BEEN on ten-hour days for only two weeks, but already he was finding it a challenge when it came to his family responsibilities. Although it was nice to have a three-day weekend, the long hours made parenting difficult.

By the time he made the commute home to Tyler every day it was after seven, which made the dinner hour sometime around seven-thirty or eight. Any leisure time was quickly gobbled up by household chores and getting Melody ready for bed.

"I'm glad I ran into you." Cece beamed with excitement as she stopped Nick outside TylerTots. "Mom told me Melody's been chosen to be Fancy's Baby. That's great!"

When Nick grimaced, she added, "Uh-oh, you don't think it's great, do you?"

They stood in front of the happy-clown sign outside the church, the evening sun creating long shadows on the lawn. Nick would have liked to forget the entire Fancy's Baby episode, but he could see the concern in Cece's eyes.

He heaved a long sigh. "I have until Friday to let them know if she's going to do it or not."

"You still have reservations?"

"A few," he answered, not wanting to rehash what had happened between him and Kika.

While they were talking, Sarah Fleming emerged from the church. She smiled and said hello, but didn't stop to talk.

As soon as the pastor had crossed the street, Cece said in a low voice, "I'm surprised she didn't stop to talk."

Nick could hear the hurt in her voice. "Have I done something I shouldn't have?" he asked.

"It's not you. It's this whole business with Michael and Jeff," Cece told him, her eyes still following Sarah's progress as she walked down Main Street.

"Michael is Sarah's husband, right?"

Cece looked at Nick and nodded. "I was hoping that he and Jeff could put the past behind them and start over, but so far they haven't been able to resolve their differences about their father."

"Jeff hasn't had much time to get used to having a brother around, has he? Annabelle said he only learned about Michael last Christmas."

"That's right, and in the meantime it's creating this strain in my friendship with Sarah."

"I'm sure it's difficult for everyone involved. My guess is that things will eventually work out. You know what they say about time—it's a great healer."

"Are you speaking from experience?" she asked him with an inquisitive lift of one eyebrow.

He shook his head. "I'm not one to be preaching. I tried for nearly two years to get over Beth's death, but it wasn't so much a matter of time, but place. I couldn't do it as long as I was living in California."

"Are you sure it's Tyler that's responsible and not Kika Mancini?"

When he didn't answer right away Cece added, "I know she spent the night at your house."

That grabbed Nick's attention. "Patrick?"

"No, Zachary. And you don't need to worry. Mom didn't hear about it."

Nick rolled his eyes. "Thank goodness. Cece, it's not what it seems—" He started to explain but she cut him off.

"Nick, you don't need to justify anything to me. I certainly don't expect you to remain single the rest of your life as a tribute to my sister."

Maybe Cece didn't expect it, but he did. "It doesn't seem right that I should be happy, not after what happened," he said solemnly.

"What are you talking about?"

"Come on, Cece. You know I was the one who wanted to have a third child, not Beth."

"And you think that because you wanted the baby it's your fault that she died?"

His silence was his answer.

"Nick, listen to me. I'm a nurse, and I can tell you that Beth might have died from that aneurysm even if she hadn't been pregnant with Melody."

"Maybe." He wanted to believe her, but guilt was a difficult burden to release.

"There is one thing I do know for sure," Cece said confidently. "Beth wouldn't want her children to be without a mother because you couldn't let go of the past."

"Kika Mancini's not exactly the motherly type," he noted with an amused chuckle.

"Not like Beth was, no, but she's not a wicked stepmother, either. The boys talk about her all the time, and it's obvious that Melody's attached to her— she named her bear after her."

Nick agreed with her but the question wasn't his children's feelings for Kika. It was whether Kika wanted to be with his children. So far, the signs weren't encouraging.

"Tell me something, Cece. If you were in my position, would you take Melody to Minneapolis to be Fancy's Baby?"

She evaded answering his question. "Melody can still be Fancy's Baby even if you decide not to see Kika again."

Maybe the modeling assignment didn't depend on his relationship with Kika, but Nick knew that if they went to Minneapolis to film the commercial, they would see Kika. Would it be wise to let his children see her again, considering how attached they already were to her?

He supposed he could always stipulate that he didn't want Kika present during the filming. That way he wouldn't have to worry about Melody wanting to get closer to her.

The problem was *he* wanted to be close to her. What disturbed him most was the possibility that Kika's interest in him would fade as soon as Melody finished the commercial. It wasn't enough that Kika wanted his daughter for Fancy's Baby. He needed Kika to want *him,* too.

So when he got back home he did the only thing he could do. He called her.

"We need to talk. Can you come to Tyler?"

IT WAS LATE by the time Kika arrived in Tyler. Street lamps lit the corners as she drove through the quiet residential area. When she turned onto Elm Street she saw the red convertible sitting in the driveway. Her heart started to pound in her chest.

It was only as she drew closer that she realized there were two cars in the driveway. Nick had company.

As Kika pulled up to the curb, the porch light went on. Within seconds, the screen door opened and out walked Cece Baron, with Nick following on her heels.

She climbed out of the rental car and walked over to them, reminding herself that Nick had invited her to come to Tyler.

"Hi, Kika. Welcome back." Cece greeted her warmly and made small talk.

Kika smiled and made all the polite responses, the whole time acutely aware of the man standing next to her. He wore a guarded look that did little to let Kika know how he felt about her appearance on his doorstep.

He said little, letting his sister-in-law do most of the talking. When she finally got in her car and drove away, Nick invited Kika inside.

"I wasn't expecting you until later," he said as he held the door open for her.

She glanced at her watch. "My flight got in ahead of schedule. Is this a bad time?"

"No, it's all right."

Zachary was playing a video game at the TV. When Nick suggested it was time to quit for the night, he asked, "How come I have to go to bed so early?"

Nick didn't respond, but simply pointed in the direction of the stairs to the second floor. With a groan,

Zachary turned off the TV. It was then that he noticed Kika's presence.

"Oh, good! You're back!"

His enthusiastic welcome warmed her heart. "Yes, and I have something for you." She set her briefcase down on the coffee table and opened it. She pulled out an eight-by-ten autographed glossy of Jim Carrey.

"Neat! Did you get him to sign it in person?"

"No, I had a friend get it for me. I have one for Patrick, too."

Zachary grabbed the second photo and went racing up the stairs, looking for his brother.

"More gifts?" Nick asked, suspicion lacing his voice.

"Umm-hmm. I have something for Melody, too. Want to see?" She wasn't going to play any games with him. She pulled out a child's tea set. "Here."

He looked at it briefly, then set it down.

"You want Fancy's Baby."

"Is Melody going to do the commercial?" She held her breath while she waited for his answer.

"I've been thinking about it," he said cautiously.

"And?"

"And I think you were right. It's too good of an opportunity to refuse. The money she earns will make a nice trust fund for college."

Kika expelled her breath all at once, then smiled. "Am I ever glad to hear you say that."

"I need to check on the kids. Can I get you something to drink while you wait?"

"No, I'm fine," she answered, sitting down on the sofa.

Footsteps pounded on the stairs and Patrick and Zachary came into the room. Melody followed behind. All three stood shyly in front of Kika, as if waiting for her inspection.

Patrick spoke first. "Melody wants to show you her lip's all better."

Before Kika had a chance to inquire about the cut, the little girl pushed her face close to hers. "It looks good," Kika said as Melody lifted her chin for examination.

"She's got something else to show you, too," Patrick added.

Melody held up her white bear and said, "My Kika."

Kika could hardly swallow, so big was the lump in her throat. "You named your bear Kika?"

She giggled shyly and nodded.

Kika reached for the tea set. "Look. I brought you something." She patted the sofa cushion beside her.

The little girl climbed up close, her eyes greedily appraising the tiny porcelain tea set. Kika wanted to brush her hands over the soft red curls, but before she had a chance to do so Nick was lifting Melody in his arms.

"Time for bed. All of you," he commanded.

Melody started to squirm and the boys groaned. "Will you be here tomorrow?" Zachary asked. The question brought an interested look from his father.

"I can come back if your dad says it's okay," Kika answered.

"Aren't you going to sleep over?" Patrick asked.

Kika felt her cheeks redden.

"Come on," Nick said a bit more sternly. "Enough with the questions." Melody continued to squirm, trying to reach Kika with outstretched arms.

"Melody wants to give Kika a hug," Zachary declared.

Kika saw Nick's eyes darken.

He bent down so that Melody could wrap her arms around Kika's neck. Before she was finished, Melody had given Kika kisses on both cheeks.

The gesture brought tears to Kika's eyes. When Nick returned from putting Melody to bed, she was dabbing at her smudged mascara with a tissue. Not wanting him to mock her affection for his daughter, she swallowed her tears and went on the offensive.

"I wanted to explain to you about the audition," she began. "It's true we didn't tape the entire list of children who came in, but that doesn't mean they didn't get consideration."

She took a deep breath and continued. "You see, it's like this. By the time we've taken a Polaroid snapshot and done a short interview, we can tell which kids just aren't going to work." As she talked, her hands moved expressively. "Instead of disappointing the parents at that stage of the game, we choose to let them believe they're being taped."

"And disappoint them later," he added in a disapproving tone.

"When you're interviewing thousands of kids, it's not an uncommon practice," she said defensively. "It saves tape and the time it takes to review the tape."

"I see."

She could tell by his guarded expression that he didn't. She needed to convince him she hadn't done it to intentionally hurt anyone.

"I didn't want to do it in Tyler, but my assistant didn't bring enough tape to start with and it seemed like a reasonable solution. And whether or not you choose to believe it, I'm not planning to do it again."

He shrugged. "It's your business."

She stood then and faced him with her hands on her hips. "Yes, it is, and frankly, I don't see why you should be so upset about this. Melody was chosen. Why does it matter to you how I run my business?"

He rose to his feet and planted his large frame directly in front of hers. "Because it's my daughter who's involved."

"You're still angry with me."

"Yes, I'm angry. You blast your way into my life—into my kids' lives—encouraging their affection, pretending you like them—"

"I do like them!" she declared emotionally.

"Is that why you left—because you'd got what you wanted?"

"I left because you didn't want me here!"

He pulled her into his arms and kissed her hungrily. "You think I don't want you?" he asked in an agonizing whisper. As if to answer his own question, his mouth covered hers in a passionate caress that left Kika in little doubt of his feelings.

Her hands reached up to cling to his shoulders as her body greeted his with the same intensity of emotion. She couldn't stop the soft moan that escaped when he ended the kiss.

"How can you possibly think I don't want you?" he asked, his eyes dark with desire.

"How can you think I don't like your kids?" she countered.

"I overheard your phone conversation that day at TylerTots." He paused, then repeated her words for her benefit. "'After this, no more kids. I just don't want to be around them.'"

With a sickening clarity, Kika recalled her conversation with her aunt Lucy. "You don't understand."

"You're right. I don't." His eyes were troubled as they stared into hers. "If you don't like kids, why are you doing everything in your power to win the hearts of mine?"

"I do like kids. The reason I said that to my aunt Lucy was because of..." She wanted to finish, but something held her back.

Fear. What if she told him about Caroline and he agreed with that nasty little voice in her subconscious that said she was to blame for what had happened?

"Because of what, Kika?" He waited for her explanation. When she didn't answer, he said, "It doesn't matter why you said it. You're important to me and to my kids." The depth of emotion in his voice touched her soul. He held her by the shoulders, his gaze pinning hers.

"When my daughter spoke her first words, it was your name she uttered. I have two sons who practically worship the ground you walk on and then there's me. I—" He stopped abruptly.

She waited for him to continue. "What about you?" she prodded gently.

"I need someone to share my life. Ever since Melody was born I've been trapped in this emotional black hole. I thought I was doing something wrong with her, that the reason she and I were struggling to have a normal father-daughter relationship had to do with the fact that her mother died at her birth.''

''And now you don't believe that?''

''I think the reason I've felt there was something missing in my relationship with Melody has to do with the fact that, emotionally, I wanted to be dead—just like Beth. Every time I looked at Melody she would remind me that I was alive. It was something I didn't want to be reminded of, until I met you.''

Her throat squeezed tight with emotion, making it difficult to swallow.

''You make me feel alive, Kika, and it's a wonderful feeling. I want to laugh and have fun. I want to go to sleep holding you in my arms and wake up to find you're still there. I know we haven't had enough time to really make this relationship work, but I believe in my heart that we're right for each other.''

He raked a hand across his head. ''That's why it's driving me crazy to think that you only used me to get to my daughter.''

''You think I only came back because I want to make sure Melody's going to be in the commercial?''

He pinned her with a penetrating gaze. ''Did you?''

''I came because I love you,'' she answered honestly, moisture gathering in her eyes.

He pulled her to him and gave her a wild, hungry kiss that had both of them breathless by the time it ended. He cupped her cheeks in his palms and said, ''Tell me this means you're not going to disappear from my life ever again.''

''I don't want to,'' she told him shakily.

He heard the uncertainty in her voice. ''I think you'd make a good mother to my children, only I'm not sure that's what you really want.''

"It is, but..."

"But what?" She tried to look away, but he held her chin firmly, forcing her to look him in the eye.

"I need to tell you something before you make any more plans." She started to tremble, so he eased her down on to the sofa, holding her just as he had that night on the Ferris wheel.

She took a deep breath. "I—I can't have children," she stuttered, then went on to tell him about Caroline and the fear she had been carrying around that she would never know what it was like to be a mother.

While she talked, he rocked her gently in his arms, softly speaking words of understanding. When she was finished, he kissed her tenderly, then said, "You can have children. You can have mine. Zachary, Patrick and Melody."

"It might take some time for all of us to adjust to one another," she warned.

"Does that meant you want to take things slowly?"

"Not too slowly." She gave him an impish grin.

"What do we do about our jobs? You work in Minneapolis and I work in Milwaukee," he said with a grimace.

"I like Tyler," she told him, enjoying the firmness of his muscles as her hand moved across his chest. "I think it would be a nice place to live."

"But what about your work?"

She sighed. "Lately I've discovered I don't have the same enthusiasm for the business I've had in the past. The huge auditions, the long hours...maybe I'm just tired, but I honestly believe it may be time for a change."

"Could you do freelance work here?"

"There is that possibility. Being we're not far from Chicago, I might be able to switch to the agenting end of the business and represent some local talents." She cuddled closer to him. "I've always been career oriented, but now I want to focus on learning a new job—how to be a mother."

He smiled and brushed a kiss across her lips. "Are you sure you don't mind moving away from your family?"

"We're not that far," she reminded him. "Besides, I will have family here. Not only will I have Fancy's Baby, I'll have her brother Zach and her brother Patrick, and best of all—" she slipped her hand around the back of his neck and pulled his head close to hers "—I'll have her father."

EPILOGUE

"GRANDMA, LOOK WHAT Kika brought!" Zachary waved a videocassette in his hands as he rushed into Annabelle's kitchen. Following close behind him was Patrick, cheeks flushed, eyes wide. "It's Melody's commercial!"

Both boys disappeared into the living room. Annabelle wiped her hands on her apron, calling out to them, "Wait for Grandma to turn on the TV."

"Knock, knock," Nick called out through the screen door.

"Come on in." Annabelle hurried over to the door, smiling at Kika and Nick as they entered the house. "So here's my fancy little baby!" she crooned, taking Melody from Kika's arms. "Let's go into Grandma's living room so we can see you on TV," she said to her granddaughter. She gestured for Nick and Kika to follow them.

"Does this mean what I hope it means?" Kika asked Nick in a whisper.

Nick squeezed her arm reassuringly. "She's the proudest grandmother in Tyler. Cece says she's passing out publicity photos to everyone who walks in the front door of the post office."

Kika saw what Nick was talking about. On Annabelle's coffee table was a stack of photos of her granddaughter.

"Nick, put the tape in for the boys," Annabelle barked in her usual manner as she sank down onto the sofa with Melody on her lap. When Kika would have taken a chair across the room, Annabelle stopped her. "Don't sit there. You won't be able to see." She patted the cushion next to her. "Come sit by us."

All eyes were on the TV as the sixty-second commercial filled the screen. The cheers that filled the room when Melody made her debut told Kika Fancy's Baby was a hit.

"I have to confess, she's perfect for the part," Annabelle declared proudly. To Kika, she said, "You do nice work, Ms. Mancini."

"Please. Call me Kika. And thank you for the compliment. I appreciate it." Kika smiled warmly at the older woman.

"It's a shame you have to quit work to move here," Annabelle commented.

"I'm not exactly quitting. In fact, after Nick and I are married, I'm going to open an office on Main Street...do some freelance agenting. Try to help those local people who want to get into commercials."

"You mean kids, right?"

"No. Talent of all ages. Even senior citizens."

Annabelle laughed. "What would they call me? Fancy's Grandma?"

Kika snapped her fingers. "That's not a bad idea . . . maybe I should give Mr. Fancy a call. . . ."

Annabelle rolled her eyes, Nick smiled and the boys giggled.

continues with

Undercover Mom

by Muriel Jensen

Daphne Sullivan and her little girl were hiding from
something or someone—that much was becoming
obvious to those who knew her. But from whom?
Was it the stranger with the dark eyes who'd just
come to town?

Available in May

Here's a preview!

UNDERCOVER MOM

"HI, DAPH!" A MALE voice called from the other side of the trail. It was Jake Marshack, Britt's husband. Walking beside him was Vic Estevez. He, too, waved.

Daphne felt a sensation like the thunder of cymbals right above her head. She wished Vic Estevez would go away. He made her nervous. She lifted Jennifer off the counter and put her back in the playpen with a book.

Another wave of customers kept Daphne busy for a considerable time afterward. By the time she had another break, the sun was lower and the crowd was beginning to thin. She leaned on the counter and looked up the trail, to see Vic Estevez walking away. His arms were wrapped around something big, obviously a recent purchase. She'd begun to wonder seriously if he was watching her. Every time she'd looked up today, he'd been there. But then so had a good number of the Tyler population. Daphne knew she had to be vigilant, but she also needed to guard against paranoia.

She went to the back of the booth to check on Jennifer—and felt panic ram into her chest like a fist. The playpen was empty! A book lay in a corner, the now empty cup of juice on top. A scruffy stuffed clown lay on its face and half-a-dozen other toys were strewn around. But there was no Jenny! The picture of Vic Estevez walking away, his arms wrapped around something, struck her. She'd been right about him. He'd been after Jenny!

VIC WANDERED in the direction of his car, assessing the day's work. Not bad. He'd made contact with the woman he was ninety-nine-percent certain was his quarry. He'd supported his cover story by—

A desperate scream rent the air and Vic stopped, not sure where it was coming from. Then something struck him from behind and an arm closed around his neck. He gripped the arm and yanked as he doubled over. His much lighter opponent sailed over his head.

Daphne Sullivan scrambled to her feet, her hair loose, her color high. She glared at him with a determination that would have put him into killer mode, had she been a real opponent.

"Where's my baby?" she screamed. "Where? Where is she?"

"I don't—" he began, and took her bony fist straight in his left eye. The blow glanced off his cheekbone and flung his head back to the dusty trail. He was grateful she was a small-boned woman.

Suddenly Britt Marshack was kneeling beside her. "No Daphne!" Daphne had grabbed Vic's shirt-front in both hands and was trying to shake him.

"Where is she?" Daphne demanded, her nose inches from Vic's. She reminded him of some beautiful-but-rabid she-cat. "Where's—my—daughter?" she repeated.

"She's here, Daphne," a soft, young voice responded. It was Christy Hansen, Britt's daughter. "I was supposed to take her at six. Remember?"

For an instant Daphne simply stared at her. Vic saw that her hands were shaking when she opened her arms to her child.

"I'd have thought a mother of two years would recognize that children do not have pink fur," Britt said, inclining her head toward the bear Vic had been holding. "I think we should get you to the first-aid booth."

"It's all right," Vic said. "I'll take her."

Britt gave Daphne an uncertain look.

"I'm fine," Daphne insisted, but he could hear the trembling in her voice.

"You look a little shocky to me," Britt said. She turned to Vic. "You promise you'll take her?"

"I promise."

The moment Britt was out of earshot, Daphne faced Vic, her expression a paradox of apology and aggression. "I can't tell you how sorry I am for accusing you of kidnapping…and for hitting you." She drew a deep breath then squared her shoulders. "But you are *not* taking me to the first-aid booth. I'm fine."

"I promised Britt."

She doubled her puny-but-powerful fist. "And I'm warning you that I'll use this again."

"When you used it before," he said quietly, "you were sitting on me, and I chose not to react because I didn't understand what your problem was. This time—" he rested his hands lightly on her hips, ready for action "—we're on even terms. Now I know you're just being stubborn."

HARLEQUIN®

I N T R I G U E®

THAT'S INTRIGUE—DYNAMIC ROMANCE AT ITS BEST!

Harlequin Intrigue is now bringing you more—more men and mystery, more desire and danger. If you've been looking for thrilling tales of contemporary passion and sensuous love stories with taut, edge-of-the-seat suspense—then you'll *love* Harlequin Intrigue!

Every month, you'll meet four new heroes who are guaranteed to make your spine tingle and your pulse pound. With them you'll enter into the exciting world of Harlequin Intrigue—where your life is on the line and so is your heart!

Harlequin Intrigue—we'll leave you breathless!

INT-GEN

BRIDE'S BAY RESORT

UNLOCK THE DOOR TO GREAT ROMANCE AT BRIDE'S BAY RESORT

Join Harlequin's new across-the-lines series, set in an exclusive hotel on an island off the coast of South Carolina.

Seven of your favorite authors will bring you exciting stories about fascinating heroes and heroines discovering love at Bride's Bay Resort.

Look for these fabulous stories coming to a store near you beginning in January 1996.

Harlequin American Romance #613 in January
Matchmaking Baby by Cathy Gillen Thacker

Harlequin Presents #1794 in February
Indiscretions by Robyn Donald

Harlequin Intrigue #362 in March
Love and Lies by Dawn Stewardson

Harlequin Romance #3404 in April
Make Believe Engagement by Day Leclaire

Harlequin Temptation #588 in May
Stranger in the Night by Roseanne Williams

Harlequin Superromance #695 in June
Married to a Stranger by Connie Bennett

Harlequin Historicals #324 in July
Dulcie's Gift by Ruth Langan

Visit Bride's Bay Resort each month wherever
Harlequin books are sold.

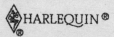

HARLEQUIN ®

BBAYG

Harlequin® Historical

If you're a serious fan of historical romance,
then you're in luck!

Harlequin Historicals brings you
stories by bestselling authors, rising new stars
and talented first-timers.

Ruth Langan & Theresa Michaels
Mary McBride & Cheryl St. John
Margaret Moore & Merline Lovelace
Julie Tetel & Nina Beaumont
Susan Amarillas & Ana Seymour
Deborah Simmons & Linda Castle
Cassandra Austin & Emily French
Miranda Jarrett & Suzanne Barclay
DeLoras Scott & Laurie Grant…

You'll never run out of favorites.

Harlequin Historicals…they're too good to miss!

HH-GEN

FIVE UNIQUE SERIES
FOR EVERY WOMAN YOU ARE...

❤ *Silhouette* ROMANCE™

From classic love stories to romantic comedies to emotional heart tuggers, Silhouette Romance is sometimes sweet, sometimes sassy—and always enjoyable! Romance—the way you always knew it could be.

SILHOUETTE® *Desire*®

Red-hot is what we've got! Sparkling, scintillating, *sensuous* love stories. Once you pick up one you won't be able to put it down...only in Silhouette Desire.

Silhouette SPECIAL EDITION®

Stories of love and life, these powerful novels are tales that you can identify with—romances with "something special" added in! Silhouette Special Edition is entertainment for the heart.

SILHOUETTE·INTIMATE·MOMENTS®

Enter a world where passions run hot and excitement is always high. Dramatic, larger than life and always compelling—Silhouette Intimate Moments provides captivating romance to cherish forever.

❤ SILHOUETTE YOURS TRULY™

A personal ad, a "Dear John" letter, a wedding invitation... Just a few of the ways that written communication unexpectedly leads Miss Unmarried to Mr. "I Do" in Yours Truly novels...in the most fun, fast-paced and flirtatious style!

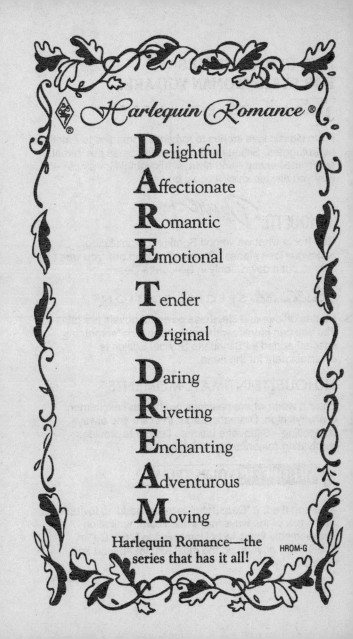

Harlequin Romance ®

Delightful

Affectionate

Romantic

Emotional

Tender

Original

Daring

Riveting

Enchanting

Adventurous

Moving

Harlequin Romance—the
series that has it all!

HROM-G